"What if I suggested we marry?"

Grace laughed again, only this time she rolled her eyes.

"I'm completely serious," Carter insisted.

"I am not getting married because of some obscure clause in your grandfather's will."

"What if I offered you two million dollars?"

"Yes please!" She immediately laughed, but then she must have seen his serious expression, because her smile and laughter faded. "I didn't mean that."

"Well, I do. You need to secure your mother's future."

"I've never once said that."

"Am I wrong, though?" Her silence was her answer. "I need a solution, and fast, and if my guess is correct, you need money."

Grace swallowed. Only now was it dawning that this really was a serious proposal...

T0197894

BRIDE UNDER CONTRACT

CAROL MARINELLI

PRESENTS

Harlequin® PRESENTS™

Recycling programs for this product may not exist in your area.

ISBN-13: 978-1-335-93913-5

Bride Under Contract

Harlequin Enterprises ULC
22 Adelaide St. West, 41st Floor
Toronto, Ontario M5H 4E3, Canada
www.Harlequin.com

Printed in Lithuania

MIX
Paper | Supporting responsible forestry
FSC® C021394

Carol Marinelli recently filled in a form asking for her job title. Thrilled to be able to put down her answer, she put "writer." Then it asked what Carol did for relaxation and she put down the truth—"writing." The third question asked for her hobbies. Well, not wanting to look obsessed, she crossed her fingers and answered "swimming"—but, given that the chlorine in the pool does terrible things to her highlights, I'm sure you can guess the real answer!

PROLOGUE

'I DON'T THINK this is going to work…' Grace Andrews was *not* talking about the faded crimson shorts she held in her hand, nor the washed-out tops that lay spread on her bed.

'They're all going to get ruined anyway.' Her friend and flatmate Violet peered at the 'essential items' list. 'You can buy new stuff after the jungle…' She paused then, and must have seen the anxiety darting in friend's green eyes. 'You're not talking about the clothes, though, are you?'

As tatty as they were, no.

Grace stood in her dressing gown, her long brown curls wrapped in a towel, her flight just a matter of hours away. There was every reason not to go.

'I should be looking for a new job. It's hardly fair on you, me working from home.'

'It makes no difference to me.' Violet shrugged. 'I'm at the library all day…' She glanced up. 'Though you are working ridiculous hours.'

'I'm used to working at night,' Grace said.

It wasn't a lie. Data entry might not sound exciting, but it had proved to be a lifeline and meant she'd been able to arrange her hours to suit as her mother's health deteriorated. But, yes, it wasn't the best pay, and certainly it wasn't going to be enough to support her mother long-term.

Grace picked up the backpack she'd been half-heartedly

packing and, clearing a space on the bed, took a seat. 'It's not just that.'

Two years ago Grace had booked and paid for a month's vacation to Malaysia, starting with a five-day river trip through the Borneo jungle. It was the most unlikely of locations for Grace, who'd never been further than a school trip to France. Only it wasn't just the sale price that had caught her attention. The stunning wildlife, as well as the luxurious river-edge villas, had enticed, but the remoteness of the jungle, along with being off-grid for a little while, had truly appealed.

The purchase had been made prior to her mum's dementia diagnosis. At the time Grace hadn't known what was wrong— just that things had changed with her mother around the time she'd turned nineteen. Eventually things had become so dire that she'd given up teacher training college and moved back home from the flat she had shared with Violet.

The holiday had been something to cling to…

She'd been purchasing hope, Grace now realised. Some sort of assurance that things would surely get better…

Only they hadn't.

Violet had been with her throughout.

They had been friends since infant school. Grace, the new girl at school after her parents' break-up, had hidden shyly behind long dark curls. She'd been in awe of the popular Violet, with her bright sunny nature that matched her golden hair. But one playtime she'd seen Violet being teased about her father being in prison.

Grace had pushed her own awkwardness aside and stepped in. 'Leave her alone!'

'What's it to you?' The lead bully had sneered.

'She's my friend,' Grace had said, taking Violet's hand.

And, apart from one regrettable incident just before her mum had been diagnosed, friends they had remained.

It had been Violet who had held Grace's hand when she'd made the heartbreaking decision to sell the family house and place her mother in a care home. And it was Violet she now shared a flat with once more, and who sat beside her on the bed and did her best to reassure Grace.

'You need this holiday—you've been dealing with this for...'

'Years,' Grace nodded.

She'd never really had time to look back and examine it.

The diagnosis had been hard, but the years prior had been their own separate version of hell.

'Maggie thinks it's a good idea if you don't visit for a while...'

Maggie, the care home's manager, had been firm, telling Grace her month's absence would give her mother the best chance to settle in.

There was a sick feeling in Grace's stomach when she thought of her mother sitting alone in the care home, waiting for her to come.

'I just don't want Mum to think she's been forgotten.'

Grace knew that feeling rather too well.

Looking out of the window...waiting for her dad's car. Running for the post on her birthday... Sometimes there *had* been a car, and he'd taken her to the fair, or to a park, but more often than not he'd failed to show up.

Finally, and without explanation, he'd stopped all contact.

'Look, I know I can't visit her...' Violet's voice trailed off.

Neither she nor Grace wanted to raise the incident that had caused their friendship to waver, when—before her diagnosis—Grace's mum had accused Violet of theft.

To this day Grace regretted her response. For a short while it had been easier to doubt her friend than accept how unwell her mother was.

'Violet...' Grace wanted to apologise properly, but Violet perhaps sensed it, because she hurriedly spoke over her.

'I promise to keep an eye. The care home's just opposite the library... I can check in with the staff... Anyway,' Violet persisted, 'you have to go. There might be some gorgeous…' She paused and gave a little grimace. 'Well, perhaps not a wildlife nerd, but once the jungle part's over and you hit the islands…'

'Believe me, romance isn't on my mind.'

'Who said anything about romance?' Violet nudged her. 'One hot night would do me. It might give me something to dream about while I'm filing the late returns.'

Though Grace laughed, she knew that for all Violet's teasing it was a bit of a front.

They were both wary of men…albeit for different reasons.

Still, lately Violet seemed more ready to shake all that off, whereas Grace felt…

She took a moment, trying to work out how she felt.

Stuck?

No, that didn't quite fit—after all she was going on holiday and her world was opening up again. The years between nineteen and twenty-five had vanished in a blur of struggling to work and care for her mum…

Lost.

It was more than that…

Grace might be sharing a flat with Violet again, but she felt so very different now than she had before.

Adrift.

Yes, that was more how she felt—adrift. As if she'd lost sight of the person she'd once been, while conversely being anchored.

She hadn't told Violet everything—possibly because she didn't want to burden her, or because she just wasn't ready for another person to know the truth. Violet thought things were fine now, but Grace knew the money wasn't going to last and could practically see the overwhelming responsibility to provide looming. Her mother was only in her fifties.

'Don't throw this holiday away,' Violet said gently.

Grace nodded, knowing better than her friend that she might never get another chance—at least not for a very long time.

A little serenity might be required!

For now, her mother was safe.

Violet's pep talk had worked and, with her mind *almost* made up, Grace glanced at the time. 'I'm going to take her in a cake and say goodbye…'

'Are you sure?'

The doubt in her friend's voice told Grace that Violet didn't think it was such a good idea.

'Won't that just confuse her even more?'

'I honestly don't know,' Grace admitted.

What she did know was that even if her mum didn't always understand, for Grace it felt important to tell her mother she loved her and to say goodbye properly.

Her father had never afforded her the same courtesy.

CHAPTER ONE

'THERE'S NOTHING FURTHER to discuss.'

Carter Bennett ended his latest brief relationship in much the same way he would abruptly terminate an unproductive meeting, or simply withdraw from what he considered a stalemate negotiation.

While he might currently be in Manhattan, the laws of the jungle had been coded into his psyche long ago.

Carter knew from bitter experience that in the jungle there were no laws—you made your own.

And now Carter had but one.

He allowed no person or place to get close.

A billionaire nomad, he had offices, properties and investments in several international locations that he moved between. As for friends—while he wouldn't describe them as such—he had a few trusted acquaintances dotted around the globe.

But not women.

There was no proverbial little black book.

Carter never left an ex on tap or on call. Be it a casual fling or a burgeoning relationship, he always severed ties completely and did so now.

'We're done.'

'You're a cold-hearted bastard, Carter.'

'Absolutely, I am,' he willingly responded. 'And that is

why I made it exceptionally clear from the start that we were going nowhere.'

He glanced at the glossy magazine on his desk that had a photo of the two of them on the cover.

He couldn't even remember the occasion.

His black hair was freshly cut, but that afforded no clue, given he had it trimmed every couple of weeks. The scar on his forehead was always visible…the suit was from his preferred London tailor… They were coming out of a theatre—but, again, that was nothing unusual. It was his preferred place to take dates.

Carter was considered a theatre buff. In truth he simply liked taking his dates there, or perhaps to the ballet or the opera. Drinks first, or a pre-performance dinner, then hours—apart from the pesky interval—without conversation.

Followed by sex.

Ironic, really, that the only photo the paparazzi had been able to find to announce their so-called engagement had Carter practically scowling. It was a stretch to say they'd even been dating, let alone about to get engaged.

'From the word go I told you I don't do relationships!' Carter tersely reminded her. 'You were the one who chose to do an interview suggesting otherwise.'

Terminating the call, he tossed the magazine into the trash.

The press on both sides of the Atlantic were having a field-day with the rumours this rather elusive bachelor was *finally* about to settle down.

Never.

Carter knew he was dead on the inside. There was a black void in his soul—one he knew could never be filled. Money, women, a new car, a night at the casino, a new abode…they brought a fleeting reprieve but, like a temporary crown, they were soon tarnished. As for settling down—Carter didn't even know what those words meant. The only thing he settled were deals. The only thing he was married to was his work as an architect.

There was nothing temporary or fleeting about the structures he helped create. They were tangible, permanent…

Lasting.

That the press was circling was nothing new—he'd lived with it all his life. Carter Bennett had been making headlines before he'd even been born into his wealthy and somewhat infamous family.

Gordon Bennett, his English father, had caused a stir in the upper echelons of society when he had called off a very suitable engagement to hurriedly marry a gorgeous and equally well-connected American socialite, Sophie Flores.

Carter being the reason!

The couple had gone on to live a bohemian life—sometimes bringing Carter along, but more often leaving him with nannies, or his eccentric grandfather in Borneo, until he'd been old enough for boarding school, where he'd thrived. He'd liked the routine, along with the education, and had shared a room with a boy called Sahir, a young prince, whose protection officer had sat outside as the young boys built ever more intricate towers and bridges.

When Carter had turned eight he'd become a big brother. It hadn't curtailed his parents' thirst for adventure and the unconventional. This time around, though, his parents had decided to 'explore as a family', and had pulled Carter from school to join them on their adventures in the jungle surrounding his grandfather's property.

Tragically, he had again become something of a sensation when he'd 'miraculously' survived an incident that had claimed Carter's parents and his baby brother.

Crocodile Attack! That had made for an excellent headline—especially when attached to the Bennett and Flores names!

Only Gordon Bennett's body had been found, and for a full

week it had been assumed Sophie and her two children had perished. But just as the story had started to fade from the front pages and screens, Carter had been back in the headlines again.

Carter Bennett Found Alive—more to come!

Details had proved sparse, though, and confusing. Somehow he'd got through infested waters and been found by local Iban people in dense jungle, some considerable distance from the river, barely clinging to life. Help was on its way, reports had said.

For Carter, help had already arrived.

He could recall opening his eyes to see his friend, Arif's father.

'*Selamat...*' Bashim had said, and gently told him he was safe. He had been able to tell in an instant that the young boy hadn't been attacked by a crocodile—his injuries had occurred in the long, lonely days after.

'Were you trying to find help?' he'd enquired gently.

But Carter had had no energy to answer.

He had a vague recollection of the motion of being carried back to Bashim's longhouse on the river's edge, and the cry of delight from Bashim's son Arif when they'd arrived. Though he'd lain there almost catatonic he had glimpses of that time—the skill and care they'd taken as they tended to his wounds, the love they'd shown to his devastated grandfather. His friend Arif, just eight himself, had held Carter's hands when the dressings on his head and back were being changed or helped him sip water.

'What did you see?' the little boy had asked, but Carter had not answered. 'Why won't he speak?' Arif had asked his papa. 'Why can't he tell us what happened?'

'Give him time,' Bashim would respond. 'He's not ready.'

To this day, those questions remained unanswered.

The empathy shown to him by Arif's family and all the

locals had been in stark contrast to what lay ahead—doctors, psychologists, investigators and his remaining family...

The press, curiously deflated that the child's injuries weren't from a crocodile, had turned its focus on what would become of the tragically orphaned boy.

For a while he'd stayed with his late father's British lawyer and his wife.

His English uncle had been in rehab and on his third marriage by then, so not really an option. And Carter's paternal grandfather refused to leave his sprawling property deep in the Borneo jungle—the same untamed land that had claimed Carter's family...

The spotlight had turned to Carter's aunt on his mother's side—a famous New York philanthropist. In truth, she'd spent far more than she'd donated, though she had clearly felt she had to be *seen* to be doing the right thing and had taken him in.

For Carter it had meant yet more nannies, but even that had proved too much for his glitterati aunt. Especially as he'd been a child who suffered with night terrors and on occasion startled the Fifth Avenue household awake!

After a couple of years appearing with her nephew on suitable occasions, with her interest waning, his aunt had shipped Carter off to England, to 'connect' with the other side of his family...

More accurately, he'd been sent back to boarding school.

A few nights of alarming his old friend Sahir's protection officer with his night terrors had quickly forced Carter to become disciplined, even in sleep, and he'd trained himself to wake up until they'd finally faded.

Most of his summers had still been taken in Borneo, though, and he'd come to dread them.

His friendship with Arif had changed. Carter had no longer wanted to go exploring with him. Arif had tried to be patient, but he'd get bored with hanging around his grandfather's luxury property. It was the rest of Wilbur Bennett's land that enthralled Arif—tens of thousands of hectares of undisturbed rainforest, not some manicured gardens and a pool.

As an adult, Carter had continued to visit.

His grandfather, always passionate about the land, had worked with the locals to preserve and monitor the rare wildlife there. Though there were still private wings to the residence, the rest of the property provided a temporary home to visiting animal scientists and researchers, as well as offices. As his grandfather had aged, Arif had increasingly taken over the running of the estate, although Carter had never had any real desire to get involved, and there had frequently been tension between the two men.

Carter had changed at a visceral level, and while Arif seemed to understand that, he refused to accept that Carter no longer wanted his friendship.

He didn't.

Carter did not want to think about losing another person he cared about to the jungle. Arif still took himself out there— not just as a guide, but to head search teams when some tourist got lost or a group went missing...

In truth, on his grandfather's death a year ago, Carter's hope had been to sever all ties to the place that had taken so much from him and still had the ability to take more.

But Wilbur Bennett's last will and testament had attempted to put paid to that.

Carter returned to his drafting desk. These days he used a lot of computer-aided design, but that wasn't going to cut it for this particular client. Crown Prince Sahir of Janana was battling with his father and elders to approve the rebuilding of a destroyed wing of the Janana Palace and had brought Carter on board. The last couple of years had been spent travelling to and from Janana. The work was intricate, even by Carter's exacting standards. Aside from that it was being challenged at every stage by the king and elders who would prefer the ruins were left undisturbed.

He couldn't quite summon his usual focus and paused for a break. Even gazing out at the Chrysler Building or the Empire State Building and admiring their architectural feats didn't work its usual magic.

It wasn't the demise of his latest relationship that was proving a distraction, his mind kept flicking to the Petronas Towers in Kuala Lumpur, and how they'd been the impetus for his chosen career.

Restless, he got up and stood gazing down on Central Park, enjoying the lush green in the middle of Manhattan where he often went for a run.

Perhaps that would clear his head?

But instead, he paced the luxurious penthouse, taking full advantage of the panoramic views. It felt more like a cage than premium office space. He looked towards the Hudson River, noting that it was sparkling and blue today. Unlike many, Carter actually preferred the days when it was brown… Though never as brown as those rivers that split the island as it meandered through the jungle… And the green of Central Park was never quite…

Well, he tried not to compare.

He chose not to compare.

Carter had done all he could to move on with his life.

But then, out of the blue, Arif had called and told him what was occurring.

'*If* you care, then you cannot turn your back.'

Carter had heard the emphasis on *if* and chosen not to address it.

He didn't want to care.

'Mr Bennett?' His PA, Ms Hill, buzzed, reminding him that Jonathon Holmes, the British lawyer who dealt with Carter's private legal affairs, was scheduled to arrive.

'Let me know when he's here,' Carter said. 'What do I have on after that?'

'An online meeting with Prince Sahir. Do you want me to set things up in the boardroom?'

'No.' Carter glanced at the plans he was working on. 'I'll take it in here.'

Glancing down, he saw that his once crisp white shirt had been marred by a couple of hours at the drawing board, so he went to the private shower and dressing room in his office to change his shirt before the meeting. Stripping off his shirt and washing his inky hands, he paused when he caught sight of his reflection. The scar that ran straight from his hairline was pale now, but it still sliced the jet-black arch of his right eyebrow in two.

Women actually liked it.

'How did that happen?' any date would inevitably ask.

But Carter would brush both the question and the enquiring hand away.

He preferred not to recall that time—and there were only small glimpses—of falling from on high, the metallic taste of iron filling his mouth, how he'd known he had to stem the bleeding...

Carter turned around and, rarely for him, craned his neck to view his back in the mirror. Possibly a little pale from way too many hours spent at the drafting desk by day, though more likely way too many late nights.

There were scars there too—although nothing like the neat gash on his face. On his shoulder and down his back the flesh was pitted, as if hot oil had been poured there. It looked as if he had gone into battle.

With barely a memory of doing it, though.

'Kalajengking,' Bashim had told him—scorpion bites.

As well as that, he'd been found unconscious on a nest of fire ants.

In regard to that fateful day he had no memory of the gory

details, and in truth preferred it that way. As for his time spent alone in the jungle…it didn't matter that he could barely recall it. The fact he'd survived should surely be enough.

Women didn't like the scars on his back quite so much, and if they inadvertently touched the scar tissue during sex he'd feel them hastily recoil.

Carter wrapped a long arm around his chest, to his back, and felt the waxy, cold flesh for himself.

No wonder they pulled away.

'Mr Bennett…?' He heard the tap on the bathroom door and Ms Hill calling his name. Thank God for their polite boundaries.

He was dressed in a matter of moments and back to his measured self.

Jonathon Holmes was as stern-faced as ever, and Carter greeted him with a handshake. 'Thanks for coming at short notice.'

'Of course.'

'How's Ruth?'

The usual pleasantries were exchanged, but the moment Carter's PA had closed the office doors he was hit with a question.

'So, are the rumours true?'

'What do you think?' Carter responded drily. 'Of course not.'

'And here I was thinking you were asking me here to draft a water-tight prenup. I'm ready for her…'

'Who?' Carter frowned.

'Whomever Mrs Bennett turns out to be.'

'Never going to happen.' Carter gave a firm shake of his head. 'I am not getting married to appease my late grandfather. What the hell was he thinking?'

His grandfather had done the unthinkable.

Ignoring Carter's cautionary words—that his cousin Benedict could not be trusted—he'd left the house and land to both his grandsons. With one proviso. If Carter married in Sabah, and remained married for a full year, he would have the option to buy his cousin out.

He seemed to have forgotten that Carter did not do sentiment in any way, shape or form, and would not be coerced into marriage.

'I warned him repeatedly that he was making a mistake…'

Carter sighed. He didn't doubt that the cutthroat Jonathon would have wanted every loose end neatly tied.

'Yet he went ahead?'

'He was always his own person.'

'True.'

While for Carter marriage was not an option, neither was he any good at fifty-fifty—especially when it came to his cousin Benedict. He'd offered to buy him out, in order to void the will, yet Benedict had not only declined, he'd put in a counter offer.

'Are you considering accepting?' Jonathon asked. 'It would be one less thing to worry about. You've got enough real estate of your own to deal with. You certainly don't need the headache of this…'

'I've heard from Arif.' He saw Jonathon's slight frown and explained. 'He co-ordinates all the research and rehabilitation projects from the property.'

'Was his father the man who rescued you?'

'Bashim.' Carter nodded, although he did not want to get into all that. 'Arif told me there's a lot of activity around the property. There are drones going up, aerial shots—'

Jonathon interrupted him. 'Benedict can't sell the property without your consent.'

'Can he lease it out, though?' Carter asked.

'There it starts to get messy, but the short answer is no.'

Carter chose not to wait for the long answer.

'Arif has heard some talk. Apparently, there are discussions underway for the location to be used as a base for a television reality show. There's also talk of a movie…'

Jonathon shook his head. 'Not without your say-so. As well as that, they'd never get permission.'

Jonathon started to launch into how tightly controlled the land was, but Carter was already ahead of him.

'Given my grandfather's standing, the officials might trust that Benedict is doing the right thing.' He told Jonathon what he knew. 'There are location scouts and television executives staying at some of the resorts.' Then Carter told him what he thought. 'I doubt they'd bother going if they didn't think there was a chance…'

'Benedict's probably relying on you backing down. He must know you can't bear—' Jonathon halted. 'Well, that you haven't been back once since the funeral.'

Carter pulled the stopper from a decanter and when Jonathon nodded poured them both a drink. But unlike Jonathon, Carter couldn't sit. He walked across his lavish office and leant his tall frame against the thick glass of the floor-to-ceiling windows, looking towards the East River now.

'If you don't want to spend the next few years fighting through the courts, then maybe it's time to let the place go,' Jonathon suggested. He didn't do sentiment either. 'It's always been a headache…you lost your parents there…'

'And my brother,' Carter reminded him, because in all this the real innocent party tended to be forgotten. 'He should never have been there in the first place.'

'No.'

It was a rare admission from Jonathon, who had handled his parents' affairs before they'd been transferred to Carter. No one had dared to speak out against the Bennetts at the time—it had been far easier to let that little detail slip from the articles.

Slip from people's minds.…

His brother's name had been Hugo, though he'd been affectionally known as Ulat. It meant worm, and was a sweet term the locals gave their newborns who, for superstitious reasons weren't named for many months. Carter, when he had been born, had been known as Ulat too.

Still, the hungry international press hadn't bothered to find out about the local ways. It had been easier to file a piece citing his father as a hero for trying to save his gorgeous wife and infant...more lucrative to focus on the miracle of Carter's survival after he'd spent a week alone in the jungle rather than query their questionable parenting choices...

Carter sorely wanted an end to his own private torture, but neither could he turn his back completely. 'Tell Benedict I'm willing to negotiate.'

'You're sure?'

Finally, with a last warning that he was being too generous, Jonathon shook Carter's hand. 'Leave it with me.'

Carter couldn't, though.

It gnawed at Carter's guts. It crept under his skin and interrupted his mind.

His gaze moved down to the busy Manhattan streets below. Yet his mind was still drifting back to Borneo. To the wild untamed rainforests...the hot, humid air that could make New York seem positively mild by comparison. He thought of the Iban people, their longhouses along big stretches of river... And then he thought of production companies, carving up the quiet waters. Sure, there were tourists, but rules were strict and the locals were both protected and protective.

'Ms Hill...' Carter buzzed his PA. 'Can you please reschedule Prince Sahir?'

Carter paused. This change of plan was something he truly didn't want.

'And if you could also clear my schedule for the week and arrange transport to Sabah.'

'When would you—?'

'Now,' Carter interrupted, rolling up the blueprints, deciding he would work on them there.

It had to be now, or very possibly he'd change his mind.

* * *

Eighteen flying hours later, Carter was at Kuala Lumpur airport.

He still wore the business suit he'd had on for a brief meeting with a financier in KL, and his tie was still immaculately knotted—albeit a little tight around his tense neck. When he was midway along the roped-off section for first-class passengers, about to board the flight that would take him to Sabah, the sight of a passport on the floor caught his attention.

Carter's first thought was that it was not his problem.

Then his eyes lifted to the potential owner, who lay dozing on an airport bench.

His second thought…

Sleeping Beauty.

No, he mentally corrected, because in the books he had long-ago read to Hugo she'd had raven-black hair and dark red lips. This woman's hair was more a glossy chestnut and her long curls tumbled off the chair…her slender hand was almost touching the floor where the passport lay.

She was, though, deeply asleep.

He went to turn to his security guard, or to Ms Hill, who usually accompanied him on business trips. But very deliberately Carter had left his entourage behind, as he always did when he reluctantly returned to the place where his demons resided. Certainly he did not bring lovers, though God knows at times he would prefer the distraction.

He walked on, saw the air stewards smiling to welcome him. And yet, glancing back, Carter saw that no one had woken her and her passport still lay there.

With an almost irritated hiss at his inability to let it go, he turned around, walked back along the roped-off section and over to the bench where the sleeping woman lay. She wore a dusky pink top and black cargo pants rather well, her slim legs were knees up, her white sneakers resting on a bag.

And, yes, she was beautiful.

Stooping his tall frame, he picked up the dark document and, meticulous by nature, checked she was the owner.

Grace Andrews was twenty-five, had been born in London, and, yes, a brief glance at the photo told Carter that indeed the document belonged to her.

He did not linger on the image long enough to take in the colour of her eyes, instead he snapped it closed.

'Madam.'

She really was deeply asleep.

'Madam,' he repeated.

He was about to move his hand to her shoulder, to rouse her, but her top had slipped, revealing a dark bra strap, and he pulled back, not wanting to alarm her.

'Ms Andrews...'

Still no reaction, so he resorted to her first name. Loudly.

'Grace!'

Green.

As her eyes slowly opened Carter found the unnecessary answer—her eyes were green.

Watching a woman awaken was a rarity for Carter.

Given his decadent history, that might appear to be a contradiction, but usually by the time morning came around Carter was turned the other way, wishing the woman away...

On occasion he was aware of lovers quietly climbing from his bed and slipping into the bathroom for a quick freshen-up. Certainly they weren't in there for extended periods. None of his lovers would do anything so crass! Instead, they quietly returned to his bed, freshly brushed and scented, eyedrops in, seemingly flawless, perfectly fake, and before he'd even opened his eyes Carter would know he'd been lied to.

Watching Ms Andrews was different.

Her beauty was unmanufactured—his experienced eyes could tell that at a glance—from the natural brows and lashes, right down to her soft, plump lips. Her face was untouched by needles or God knows what else, and her pale skin wore not a scrap of make-up. For a brief moment, as she woke, two utterly perfect crystals met his, her pupils constricting in the light, revealing ever more of verdant mossy green, and if eyes really were the windows to the soul he could have sworn she was smiling at him.

But then the real world impinged.

He watched confusion start to flicker in her eyes, followed by a flutter of panic. Like a kaleidoscope twisting in reverse, the prisms shattered as she took her gaze from him and glanced at her surroundings, a frown appearing, the clear green fracturing, her soft smile fading as she abruptly sat up, her top slipping down further, her hair a chaotic tumble...

'It's fine,' Carter reassured her.

Grace didn't hear him, though.

She'd woken to find a stranger standing over her.

A black-haired stranger, with a clean-shaven strong jaw, a straight Roman nose. But what drew her attention was the perfect separation of his left eyebrow—a thick white scar cut through the gorgeous jet arch and into his hairline. His eyes were as grey as sleet on a cold winter's day, and he had a stern, grim, yet somehow plump and completely kissable mouth. His stance might be construed as forbidding, yet there was no sense of threat. The citrussy, spicy scent of his cologne and its smoky undertone was so delectable, so real, it took away from the hard bench beneath her body and the harsh lights behind him...

In truth, for a moment, when their eyes had first met, she'd *welcomed* him to step into her dream.

Then it had dawned on her that this was no dream! The stranger her eyes had beckoned to join her was real...

The sounds of the airport seemed muffled and lost to her senses as she first took in his features, then looked to his proffered hand and saw she must have dropped her passport.

'Gosh!' Grace hauled herself to sit up and glanced around.

The departure lounge that had been nearly empty when she'd given in to exhaustion and closed her eyes to doze was now full. She glanced at the screen and saw that first-class passengers had already been invited to board.

'I must have…'

He proffered the passport again and, orientated now, she reached to take it. Grace saw the glint of an expensive watch and crisp white cuffs beneath the sleeve of a dark grey suit, and even his hands were immaculate, right down to his manicured nails.

'Goodness…' she said, closing her hand around the passport that must have slipped from her pocket. 'Thank you.'

He said something, but his voice was barely audible, his words just a deep, indecipherable burr.

'Sorry?'

She asked him to repeat. His voice did not match his impact. His words were so faint that she was forced to look at his mouth to make out what was being said.

God, those lips, she thought. For even if he appeared to be forming stern words they remained full and plump.

But now, when he pointed his index finger in slight rebuke, she caught what he said.

'You should be more careful.'

Grace was about to tell him that usually she was…boringly careful. But Mr Stern was already walking on.

Coming to fully, she thought of his wagging finger and felt both foolish for dropping her passport and also a bit cross.

To his departing back, and under her breath, she muttered a quiet, 'Yes, sir!'

Or rather, Grace *thought* she had muttered—but, watching his shoulders stiffen before he abruptly turned around, she realised he'd somehow heard.

He shot her such a look that Grace swallowed hard. So hard it caused a sudden popping noise in her ears, followed by a voice over the Tannoy calling for *'passengers requiring assistance'* to board.

The world instantly got louder.

There were people all around, talking, babies were crying, and Grace realised that the aeroplane ear she hadn't known she had must have suddenly rectified.

And it dawned on her that very possibly she'd been shouting!

'My ears…' She pointed her fingers to the problem. 'I couldn't hear myself…'

He must think her mad, Grace decided. Soon he would walk over and tell her that next time she could take care of her passport herself…

It came as a ridiculously nice surprise when his sulky mouth moved into a slight smile. A smile that told her she was forgiven. Better still, this austere man seemed vaguely amused.

'Thank you,' she said again, hopefully a little less loudly than last time, and he gave her a brief, polite nod before moving on.

He was carrying a long leather cylinder and a laptop bag, and she watched as he walked along the VIP section towards the smiling flight attendants. And then her moment with the beautiful stranger was gone for ever.

Gosh, Grace thought, her heart hammering—not just at the near miss with her passport, but more at the impact of him.

She tried to shrug the brief encounter from her mind and looked around at her fellow passengers, who barely deigned to give her a glance.

She checked her phone messages and listened to Violet wishing her a safe trip. Then she felt the familiar knot of anxiety tighten as she opened her emails. It was merited, because there was the July invoice for her mother's first two weeks in the nursing home.

It would already have been debited, so she could easily ignore it, and there was a part of her that wanted to wait until after her holiday. To simply escape the issue for a while...

Hairdresser...

Manicure...

Group Trip...

Gardening Club...

Grace closed her eyes.

Those were the exact things she wanted for her mother, but the top-up fees were beyond anything she'd remotely envisaged.

Her mind was still on the blasted account as she boarded, but as she waited for the flight attendant to check her boarding pass Grace let her gaze drift to the left, possibly hoping to see the delectable stranger. She peered at the business class cabin and saw the champagne being taken around, though there was no sign of him.

A curtain was pulled back and she glanced beyond and briefly glimpsed a flash of a white shirt and a glint of a gold watch, then a jacket being handed over, before the curtain was abruptly closed.

He was beyond business class, and somehow she'd already known that.

That stunning, prepossessing man was beyond anything she'd ever seen.

He was simply *beyond*.

CHAPTER TWO

SERENITY?

Not quite…

Even so, sitting in the boat with her fellow travellers, Grace had certainly caught a few glimpses of it. In witnessing Mother Nature at her finest, there were times she had to pinch herself to believe she was really here.

It had been the most incredible few days. Sunrise boat trips followed by a gorgeous breakfast with her group, then a day to explore the boardwalk around the gorgeous resort. Or simply to rest on a lounger and watch the gentle activity on the river. Or relax in her suite.

After several turbulent years, finally there had been time to reflect and think—about her mother, her future, how wonderful Violet had been.

And there had been time to daydream…to lie in a hammock and think about gorgeous strangers who stared right into your eyes. How he'd smiled…

Today, before dusk, the ten in her party had set out again, to watch the animals and birds prepare for the night ahead. While she still hadn't seen orangutans, tonight had been a highlight—on their way back they'd had to stop the narrow open boat as pygmy elephants crossed the river.

They were not so small…

Night was closing in as the exhilarated group made their way back, the lights of the villa twinkling invitingly ahead.

'We're rather late,' Felicity, their extremely efficient guide for the evening, reminded them. 'So get changed for dinner as quickly as possible.'

Guests were expected to dress for dinner, and on the day Grace had arrived a red sarong shot with silver had been waiting on her bed. At first it had felt strange to dress up, but Grace had started to enjoy how seriously meals were taken here. A gong would summon the guests to a stunning alfresco dining area set high over the river. There the guests would sit in their allocated groups and share in a sumptuous buffet dinner.

Mindful that they were running late, Grace had a very quick shower, then ran a comb through her newly wild hair—the humidity hadn't been kind. Her long curls seemed to have doubled in volume and her comb kept snapping off teeth. Giving up on taming it, she tied it up in a messy bun—and then it was time to tackle the sarong.

Grace headed out, walking through the softly lit grounds to the gorgeous alfresco area, slipping off her shoes before entering.

'Hey, Grace...'

One of the group, Randy, greeted her, as did everyone else, but then they all got back to their conversations.

Selecting a fragrant dish, Grace took a seat at the table. As much as she was loving her time here, she did feel like the odd one out. She knew she was out of practice socially, and her attempts at conversation and even her little jokes all seemed to fall on deaf or bemused ears.

Most in the group were considerably older—retired or semi-retired couples—and were well travelled. There were a few younger ones—a couple on their honeymoon and Corrin, who was German and a keen photographer. The only thing Grace had to take pictures with was her rather basic phone...

'Wow!' Randy was looking at some stunning footage Corrin had taken, and they were speaking about apertures and such.

Possibly, Grace thought as she selected dessert, she'd put herself a little on the outside right from the start. When they'd first introduced themselves she hadn't really wanted to admit how worried she was about her mum, so had been vague with her responses, and had perhaps sounded standoffish—which hadn't been her intention.

Grace was eating some fruit, the meal almost over, when Randy glanced towards the entrance and rolled his eyes.

'Late as always...'

She knew who he was referring to—a loud group who neither changed for dinner nor removed their shoes.

'I swear they're developers,' Randy said, standing up, as did his wife. 'Enjoy the peace here while you can—it won't last long if they get their hands on it...'

He wished everyone goodnight and left.

'Do you think they are developers?' Grace asked Corrin.

'They are not interested in much.' Corrin shrugged and, collecting her camera, told Grace she was going to bed. *'Ich geh ins bett.'*

'Sleep well.' Grace smiled.

Given the early-morning starts, they all seemed to drift off to bed about nine. Well, except for the newlyweds, who played Uno every night! For Grace, having spent the past couple of years working late into the night, as well as keeping an ear out for her mother, it felt a little early for the day to be over.

She wandered from the dining area, happy to be away from the obnoxious group that had just arrived. Not quite ready for bed, she took a chair beside a low table close to the walkway. There was no internet or phone signal, but Grace scrolled through her phone, trying to find the footage she'd taken tonight.

'Watch out for the monkeys!' Felicity warned as she passed. 'I'll see you bright and early...'

* * *

It was dark and late as Carter approached the resort.

He slowed the speedboat as he passed the longhouses, so as not to disturb the Iban people, as was the custom here.

Usually he arrived at his grandfather's by helicopter, but he had arranged for his speedboat to be waiting and had travelled by river. He'd made several stops along the way, both at the resorts and sharing meals with the locals, finding out all he could before meeting with Arif. After this he would travel on to his late grandfather's, but soon, Carter hoped, he could head back to the States—or Janana, given the last-minute cancellation of his meeting with Sahir.

Pulling in to the jetty, he stared at the dark stretch of river beyond, thinking of the turn-off a few miles ahead and the network of tributaries to negotiate before he came to the part of the world he hated the most.

'Carter!'

As he secured his boat Jamal, Arif's wife, came down the stairs to greet him.

'Welcome…we heard you were back.'

'Word travels,' Carter agreed.

'I haven't seen you for so long. Not since the funeral.' Jamal met his eyes then. 'I can't even remember the last time you visited us here at the resort.'

She pushed out a smile, but he could see the worry behind it.

'A suite is ready for you, of course, though Arif is not here right now. He's taking a night group out, but he'll be back by morning.'

'That's fine.'

He was actually relieved to avoid heavy topics tonight, as well as the ongoing tension between himself and Arif. Instead, he asked about the couple's young children, and found out the eldest was out in the jungle with his father tonight.

'Already?' Carter frowned, appalled at the thought of a child out there. 'Reheeq's only four...'

'He's six—and you went out long before then.' Jamal laughed. 'Here...' She gave him a key. 'Do you want dinner while your luggage is unloaded?'

'I'm fine,' Carter declined. 'I've had a lot of stops along the way.'

'Then I'll show you to your suite...'

'No need.' Carter knew the place like the back of his hand.

'It's good you're here,' Jamal said, then glanced up from the little jetty to the softly lit dining area above. 'I had better go...there are still guests dining...'

She dashed off, which in itself was unusual for Jamal, but walking down the walkway he heard rather raucous laughter from the dining area and knew she must be busy.

For most the resort was a tranquil paradise, with trailing flowers, the sound of cicadas... But for Carter, being back was his own version of hell. The dense jungle was not just close, it shrouded the resort and—call it denial—he would by far prefer not to have known that Arif and his young son were out there tonight.

But then from dark thoughts there was a sudden and very unexpected distraction.

It would appear that Grace Andrews, the woman from the airport, was staying here at the resort.

Carter recognised her immediately—recalled her name instantly. He'd even thought about her on the flight. Flying at altitude, cabin lights dimmed, he'd found that he'd smiled when recalling their brief interaction, and how she'd blushed when he'd overheard her calling him 'sir'.

Now her beauty, even in the dim lighting, was almost luminescent, and his eyes were instantly drawn to where she sat on a large chair, with her legs tucked under her, looking through her phone. She was wearing a red sarong, revealing slender arms and shoulders, and her hair was tied high in a loose knot. She was alone.

'How are the ears?' he asked, and watched her jolt.

'Oh!' she said as she looked up. 'It's you.'

Then she smiled, her full lips spreading, as did the pink tinge to her creamy complexion. She smiled not just with her eyes, as she had so briefly at the airport, and not just with her lush lips, but with her whole self.

Putting down her phone and uncurling her legs, she sat up.

For Carter the initial impact he'd felt on sighting her was followed by two counter punches—one to his groin, as his body reacted to her effortless beauty in a familiar way, and also a rare hit to his chest, a surge of pleasure simply to see her warm smile. Though he doubted Grace could begin to comprehend just how welcome her greeting was at this intolerable time.

'My ears are much better, thank you.'

He watched as she tucked loose tendrils of hair behind little pixie-looking ears. After a difficult few days Grace really was a sight for sore eyes. Oh, there had been no hostility on his journey—the locals were too kind and welcoming for that. It was more that he'd been able to feel their concern, and a slight air of suspicion also—which, given it was his cousin who posed the danger, he knew was merited.

Yes, Grace Andrews was a pleasant surprise indeed.

'Your voice is a lot…' He paused before selecting his word, thinking how loud it had been when he'd woken her. It was gentler now, as well as a little throaty and… 'A lot softer than I recall.'

And all the huskier for seeing you! Grace thought, clearing her throat, while wondering what on earth had happened to her vocal cords.

He was as stunning as she'd remembered him to be. And, yes, when recalling their first meeting she'd wondered if she'd somehow exaggerated his beauty. But if anything she'd under-played it. He wore a dark, untucked yet fitted shirt, with the sleeves pushed up, and grey linen trousers. He was unshaven and sporting several days' worth of dark stubble. But even casually dressed, even with that black hair a touch dishevelled, he cut an expensive dash.

'All alone?' he asked, glancing down at the single iced tea on her table.

'Yes. Well, except for the newlyweds and...' She gestured with her head to the noisy group in the dining area behind.

'Are they in your tour group?'

'No, thank goodness.' Grace shook her head. 'They got here before us. I think they're...' She halted, certain he didn't want to hear her musings, but it would seem she was wrong.

'Mind if I join you?' he said, gesturing to the empty seat opposite.

'Of course not.'

'Do you want a drink?' he offered. 'I'm going to find some wine.'

'I'd love one—though I doubt you'll have much luck. I think there's only beer.'

'I'll see what I can do.'

As he sauntered off she briefly closed her eyes, warning herself not to read too much into him joining her. It wasn't as if he could be spoiled for company! She had to somehow ignore just how gorgeous he was and her almost violent attraction to him.

She took a deep breath, deciding to examine this moment later.

This moment when her heart felt like a trapped butterfly in her throat.

This moment when she was still fighting the surge of adrenaline that had made her want to leap from her seat the second she saw him—like some overgrown puppy.

She opened her eyes to the sight of him returning with a

bottle of wine and two glasses. He gave a slow smile of tri-
umph as he held up the bottle, and it felt as if she was the only
woman here.

Well, she *was* the only woman sitting alone here, Grace
reminded herself.

Yet somehow, holding her in his gaze, he made her feel a
little as if she was the only woman in the world.

Oh, yes, it would be far wiser to dwell on his impact later.
These feelings he evoked were unfamiliar.

Tantalisingly so…

Carter pulled out the cushioned chair opposite Grace, ensur-
ing a clear view of his target—the group of men in the dining
area didn't look like regular tourists.

'I feel at a bit of a disadvantage,' Grace admitted as he sat.

'How so?'

'Well, you saw my passport, so you know my name, my
age, where I'm from…'

'Ah, but I have a terrible memory,' he teasingly lied. Then,
while opening the bottle, told her all he had gleaned. 'Grace
Andrews, twenty-five, born in London, though I didn't get
your date of birth.'

She laughed lightly, though her green eyes waited and if he
wanted to observe these men, then he'd have to give up more.

'Carter,' he offered, 'Carter Bennett.' He briefly glanced
over to the group as he poured the wine. He was excellent
at mining information and decided to utilise that skill now.
'God, they're loud,' he commented, leading the conversation
back to where she'd left it a short while ago. 'Usually everyone's in bed by now, or winding down—they seem to be just
getting started…'

'Mmm…' She shrugged creamy shoulders, then, rather
than elaborating on the group, asked about him. 'You didn't
say how old you were.'

'Thirty-five.' He chose to be more direct. 'So, who are they?'

'I've no idea.' She shook her head. 'Randy, one of the guys in our group, heard them discussing building an airstrip. He thinks they might be developers, or something.'

Carter at first made no comment, but he was rather sure he knew who they were now—they weren't developers, they were television or movie executives wanting easier access to the residence and land. He needed to observe them some more to be certain. While inviting a tourist to regale their adventures was something he'd usually avoid, he was rather brilliant at feigning interest when it was to his advantage. 'How are you enjoying your trip…?' he enquired politely.

'Very much.' She nodded. 'It's gone by too fast…just a couple more days here…'

'Then what?'

'I still haven't made up my mind,' Grace told him as, rather than sliding it across the table, Carter handed her a drink.

Grace took it a little tentatively, hoping her hands weren't too slippery from a mixture of both the humidity and her own jangled nerves, but he held the glass securely until she had a firm hold.

It was the tiniest thing, really, but she was grateful that he at least was entirely in control. Or perhaps it was just that the brief touch of their fingers and fleeting contact hadn't affected him in the slightest.

Of course not.

'Really, I'd be happy to stay on a little longer,' Grace admitted. 'I'd love to see orangutans.'

'You haven't yet?'

'A nest, and one from a distance, though I'm dreadful with binoculars.' She gave him a smile. 'Seeing orangutans has been on my bucket list since before I even knew what bucket lists were…'

'How come?'

She blushed, and it was something she tended not to do.

Or maybe she did—she'd just never been so conscious of it until she met him.

'It's silly…' she dismissed her reasoning. 'My father got me a baby one for Christmas when I was little. Not a real one…'

'I would hope not! I've heard they do terrible damage to curtains.'

She smiled at his subtle humour, and then it turned into a laugh, and his company was so pleasant, even if there was still heat in her cheeks.

'You can send him a photo of a real one soon.'

'I don't think so…'

'You'll see plenty if you go to one of the rehabilitation centres—'

'I meant, we're not in contact.' She gave a tight smile and got back to talking about the orangutans. 'They've always fascinated me. I'd just love to see one in the wild.' Before he could say it, she put up her hand. 'I know. Felicity has already reminded me it's not a zoo.'

'Felicity?'

'One of the guides,' she explained. 'I believe she's here doing research. Ornithology,' Grace added. 'Anyway, seeing orangutans in the wild is probably not all I've built it up to be…'

He opened his mouth, as if about to say something, then must have changed his mind and closed it. But as she went to take a sip of her wine perhaps he changed his mind again. 'Grace, it's even better.'

'Oh…'

Her surprise wasn't at his comment, more at the slight husk to his voice, the note of pensiveness, even. But then he gave a casual shrug, as if it might reduce the sentiment of his words.

She narrowed her eyes as she looked at him. 'You're not here on a tour…'

'Is it that obvious?'

She shrugged. 'You just seem…' Her head moved to one

side in slight assessment. 'Well, you arrived alone, *and* you know where the wine's kept.'

He gave a half-laugh. 'My grandfather has—or rather he *had* a place a few miles from here.'

She blinked, and he knew she had noticed the change of tense when he'd mentioned his grandfather.

Please don't offer condolences, he thought, but she just briefly met his eyes and a gave him a pinched, regretful smile that said enough.

Actually, it said more—it told him that she'd heard, or rather understood, he'd rather not go there.

'So,' Grace summed up, 'not a tourist, but not a local either?'

'Correct.'

He was grateful she'd changed the topic, and he rested his eyes upon her as she told him they'd all seen the pygmy elephants tonight.

'Just incredible...'

There was a tremor of excitement in her voice, and he found his focus honing in on her, the men in the dining area forgotten as her delicate hands reached for her phone.

'I took some photos, and I think I got a couple of videos. I was about to look when you...' She paused, and then got back to searching on her phone.

Carter was not one for tourist photos—or any photos. Usually someone reaching for their phone would have him reaching for his wine, or the exit—and yet as she held up a grainy image on an utterly basic phone Carter found out something.

It wasn't just elephants that didn't forget.

There was a twist inside him, a whisper of long-ago carefree days spent tracking them with Arif. How everything would halt when they chose to appear by the river—even seasoned locals could not but stop and smile at their majesty.

His father had been in constant awe of them too.

'Carter, look!'

It had been more than half a century since he'd recalled his father's voice with such clarity.

Not that Grace could know that, of course.

'It really was the most incredible thing I've ever...' she started but then halted, perhaps changed her mind, because she went to place her phone back down on the table. 'You must have seen them a thousand times.'

He was about to nod, even if only to halt the memories raining in, yet he didn't want to crush her fervour nor shut it down. Also, for the first time, there was no pain in recall.

'Not for a long while,' Carter admitted, standing to move his seat around to be by her side. The men he'd intended to watch—the very reason he was here—were forgotten.

'This was earlier...' Grace told him, and he tried to look down at the phone rather than notice the dash of coral polish on her toenails. 'We first saw them by the river.'

His gaze left her pretty feet to look at the images, and there was something about the photos lack of polish that made there really rather special.

'That's quite a herd,' he commented.

'Eleven...maybe twelve.' She nodded, and he caught the scent of fragrant hair and warm skin. 'And there was a calf,' she added. 'Well, two. But one was just so tiny. This was taken at the start.'

She showed him a very shaky video, and he looked at the elephants at the riverside, their silvery ears flapping as if waving, carrying on eating and bathing, oblivious to their audience.

God, but he remembered this.

Carter was certainly not one for poring over holiday images, and such, yet he patiently watched her slender finger as she swiped through more photos, the sky darkening with each image.

'We were heading back to the resort when they appeared again. I don't think Felicity was expecting it at all! We had to stop to let them cross.'

He could hear the tremor of excitement in her voice.

'It was getting dark, so you can't see much...'

'May I?'

He took the phone and watched the footage, heard her laughter in the short video. It moved him. Her slight gasp as another elephant appeared, followed by her cry of delight as a small calf disappeared beneath the water.

The dulcet notes of her pure pleasure were captivating.

'I didn't even know they could swim,' she admitted, her head moving closer to his, a curl just dusting his cheek. 'And then...'

Together they watched as one of the mothers pushed her little one up onto the muddy bank and the elders stood patiently, waiting for all to gather.

'They really take care of each other.'

'They do.' Carter said. 'Once, I thought...'

He halted—not just his voice, but his thoughts—as he always did when his mind drifted back. Yet as he stared at the images on the phone her silence was patient enough to allow him a small recollection of happier times.

'Once, I thought I'd found an abandoned calf.'

'Oh, my goodness. What did you do?'

'Nothing—luckily. Arif intervened, told me the herd were close. It could have turned nasty—they weigh in the tons.'

'Arif?' Grace checked. 'The guide here?'

He nodded.

'Thank goodness for friends.' She laughed, but then it trailed off. 'I almost didn't come... I cancelled this trip a few times. But my friend Violet practically marched me to the airport.'

She didn't elaborate, and Carter found he wanted her to.

Grace had found out something too—the inescapability of desire.

They were both looking down at her now blank phone, and she was suddenly utterly aware that he sat close to her. She could see his long, lean thigh next to hers, and his beautiful fingers holding her phone, the sorts of things she'd never really noticed in a man before…

Since that first meeting at airport she'd been doing her level best to get him out of her mind, and now he'd arrived at the resort she was trying to treat him just as she would any of her fellow travellers.

Yet for all her denial, for all her bravado, her heart—which had barely slowed since his arrival—picked up pace again. And when their fingers brushed as he handed her back the phone, the butterfly in her throat felt like a trapped, panicking moth.

'Thanks,' Grace said, placing it on the table and wondering if he'd move his chair back now. But he remained by her side, which meant they had to turn a little to face each other. 'It's nice to show someone.'

'Aren't you all swapping photos at dinner?'

He clearly knew the resort well. 'I don't really…' She didn't know how to say that she didn't quite fit in—it wasn't a flattering thing to admit. 'They're mainly couples.'

'Yes?'

'And I'm not the best photographer…'

'I liked your pictures.'

'Thank you.' She rolled her eyes, but then her gaze went straight back to his. 'They don't get my jokes either. Mind you, they're pretty dreadful.'

'I'll try and remember to laugh.'

Carter didn't look like a man who laughed very often, and yet he made her smile with rare ease. More, there was a gentle yet particular attention he gave.

As if he even registered her blink.

Certainly she noticed when he did—the bat of his spiky black lashes and then the captivating return of a slate-grey that seemed to set the world into slow motion.

Her reaction was heightening—more now than just a faint

blush or a fluttering heart. There was a pleasurable air of light tension. Her breasts, her stomach, and even lower felt subtly… provoked. Stirring, stretching, tuning up like the orchestra at the start of a concert…or rather tuning in to new sensations. She had never felt such attraction, and most bewildering of all, for Grace it felt reciprocated.

As if Carter felt it too.

Of course not, she told herself, reaching for her wine, determined to appear unaffected. It wasn't just that he was out of her league, or that he was out of her realm, it was the fear of misreading him. The fear that it was woeful inexperience that had her misinterpreting the static air between them.

He took a drink, drained his glass, and her eyes flicked to his mouth as his pink tongue lightly licked his bottom lip.

Such a simple motion, yet Grace found herself, both entranced and determined to act as if she hadn't noticed.

Grace tried to deny she was, for the first time, on fire.

CHAPTER THREE

'So…' CARTER NOTICED Grace pushing out a smile and retreating from their silent flirt. 'You're visiting your grandfather's home?' she asked.

For a moment there he'd thought they might kiss, pick up his key and head to bed…

It was that easy for him.

Yet, as pleasurable as an escape would be, he wasn't here for that.

And also he was enjoying their conversation.

Unexpectedly so.

'Yes.' Carter nodded.

He rarely discussed personal matters, yet here he was, sitting above the river, dragged back to a world he'd hoped to avoid. And he'd never see her again.

'He left his estate to both my cousin and I.' He gave a small grimace and she must have noted it.

'You don't get on?'

'We don't,' he agreed, topping up their glasses. 'I have no idea what my grandfather was thinking. He must have been losing his mind.'

'Please don't—'

She put up a hand, her voice still soft, but passionate and urgent. Enough so that he put down the bottle.

'Sorry…' She seemed embarrassed to have halted him. 'I

just hate that turn of phrase. My mother actually *is* losing her mind.'

'Then I apologise for my careless words.'

'It's fine.' She shrugged tense shoulders, took a breath, and he watched her force them to relax. 'I shouldn't have said anything.'

Grace didn't really know why she had.

For days she'd actively avoided the topic, and though she'd started to regret holding back from the group it felt too late now to amend that. But with Carter there was a certain allure in his grey eyes. Or perhaps, sitting there on a sultry night, surrounded by a sky hung with stars, it was easier, just for a short while, to let down her perpetual guard.

'When you say she's losing her mind…?'

Grace would never get used to saying it, and her lips were tight around her words. 'She has dementia.'

'She must be young?'

'Yes. She's just gone into a nursing home. A nice one,' she added, deciding she'd said enough—it was hardly gentle conversation.

'How long has she been unwell?'

Grace hadn't expected the question. She looked at eyes that, colour-wise, remained as cold and grey as a winter's day, yet she felt as if she sat by a fire, the world outside a window, all the warmth and comfort here.

'A few years…'

She'd been thinking back on it earlier, as she'd lain on the hammock. 'I never even considered it at first.' She saw…not a frown, more his eyes narrowing in a kind of interest. And maybe it was the wine, or maybe this week had given her space, because for the first time she felt able to examine those bewildering times.

'She became…' How best to put it? 'Tricky.'

'I am guessing that's an understatement?'

'Not at first.' Grace shook her head. 'It was hard to pinpoint, I just knew something was wrong. I tried to rationalise it…' She gave a pale smile. 'Ignore it.'

'Did the rest of your family notice?'

'It's mainly just us. There's an aunt and cousin, but they didn't think anything was amiss…' Grace said. 'I was sharing a flat with my friend Violet, and I moved back home. I didn't tell her why.'

'How come?'

'There are some things that you just don't share.' Grace thought back. 'Things you don't want others to see. Well, that's how it felt for me.' She looked at him. 'I felt disloyal, maybe?'

He frowned, as if deeply considering her words. For a moment she thought he had a question, or was about to say something, but he stayed silent.

'Then she accused Violet of stealing a necklace.'

'That was the tipping point?'

'No.' Grace swallowed before adding. 'Unfortunately not.'

She'd stopped crying a very long time ago, but this memory was one of the few things that could almost reduce her to tears.

'I didn't accuse her…but I didn't defend her as I should have.'

The cicadas were silent, as if they too were listening, but then a loud burst of laughter from the group of men snapped her back to the present.

'It was the impetus to talk to our family doctor.' She met Carter's very accommodating gaze. 'When I was first told all I worried about was that it might be hereditary.' She was past putting herself in a flattering light. 'How selfish is that?'

'Practical, maybe?' Carter suggested. 'I'd want to know.'

'Well, her type of dementia isn't, as it turned out.' She thought for a moment. 'It's just a cruel disease…'

'Was her illness the reason you cancelled your trip?'

Grace nodded. 'I was her carer—and working too, of

course. But I was lucky enough to be able to do my job from home…data entry…'

'So, you were doing two jobs?'

'I'm not sure taking care of my mother counted as a *job*.' She frowned at his rather direct summing up. 'And as well as that I would never have…' She paused, that disloyal feeling revisiting her. No, she would not be discussing her mother's finances. 'Well, if I'd known all that was coming, I wouldn't have planned a month away.'

'But now she's being taken care of?'

'Yes…' She wavered, knowing he couldn't possibly get the pain behind her choice. But neither did he *need* to know, so she forced a smile. 'There's a choir group, gardening…she's got a better social life than I have!'

He didn't return her smile. Only it didn't feel as if another of her little jokes had fallen flat—instead, it was as if he was giving her a pause before elaborating.

But she was already a little stunned that she'd told him so much.

This stranger.

Who magnetised her…who'd drawn thoughts out of her like iron filings…

She felt embarrassed by how much she'd said. 'Sorry for oversharing.' She grimaced. 'I haven't told anyone here. This place, though…' She looked out to the river and the sky above. 'It makes you slow down.'

'And, of course, there's no internet,' he pointed out.

'True!' She glanced up as the newlyweds passed and said goodnight. 'Sleep well.' Grace said.

'Newlyweds?' he checked.

She nodded.

He frowned. 'Playing cards?'

I know! Grace wanted to say, because she'd thought exactly the same.

She didn't go there, though—after all, she had no sex life to compare.

However, if she were on her honeymoon...with someone as...

'I ought to get to bed.' She put down her glass. 'We're meeting at dawn. Last chance to see the orangutans!'

'Good luck,' Carter said, and put down his glass too. 'I'll walk you back to your villa.'

'There's really no need—it's just there.'

It was literally ten or so steps away, but he looked at her as if there were things she did not know.

'There's every need,' he responded. 'We have company.'

He nodded towards the fence that lined the route to her door and she jumped a little when she saw a group of macaque monkeys, sitting happily observing them.

'I didn't even notice.' She gave a nervous laugh and watched as he picked up their glasses and bottle.

'They can cause a lot of havoc in one night,' he explained, then left her to return the bottle and glasses to wherever he'd located them.

So could he, Grace thought, popping her phone into her bag as she awaited his return.

An hour in his company, immersed in those grey eyes, and her head was in disorder, thrown completely off balance by her own reaction to this intriguing man.

And, while she'd terminated their night, it had nothing to do with not enjoying his company. And certainly it wasn't because of her early start in the morning.

Quite simply, she was desperate for order to be restored.

For the fire he seemed to have lit inside her to be doused.

'It's that one,' she said, pointing to her villa, and he walked her the short distance, the curious monkeys observing them as they arrived at her door.

'It was nice seeing you again, Grace.'

'And you.' Grace nodded and went for her key.

Then she looked up at him.

More than nice.

And despite her previous need to conclude things, now that the moment was here she was suddenly desperate for more of this disorder, desperate to explore these new sensations, to know his kiss.

Possibly her eyes revealed some of her thoughts, for his fingers took a stray strand of her hair and tucked it behind her ear. His direct touch came as a relief rather than a shock. It felt like tangible proof that the attraction was mutual—that she wasn't imagining that someone so suave and gorgeous might be desirous too. His palm remained, and rather than brush his hand away, she lingered in the bliss of the slight, lightly provocative touch, wanting to arch her neck to rest into it.

'Unexpected,' she added.

'Nicely so,' he agreed.

Her nerves felt as if they were wound tight enough to snap, yet there was also a low beat of excitement…like distant drums. Did he know this was her most thrilling moment? That standing here, miles from anywhere, bathed in stars and touched by him, she was feeling the most peace, the most excitement she'd ever known? And it wasn't the cruel shelter her mother's disease had caused that had kept sensation at bay. Nothing had ever come close to the thrill of his company, his touch. And if she knew how, she would step into his kiss, or lift her face…

Carter was sorely tempted to lower his head and taste that ripe mouth. More than tempted. He wanted to gather that slender body and hold it against his, to sink into familiar escape with this captivating beauty…

She wasn't used to this, though—he was experienced enough to tell that.

There had been two chances to move their conversation to bed and she'd refused them both.

Now, though, he felt her warm cheek, saw that full, waiting mouth, and he knew where it would surely lead.

And she'd regret it.

Not the night, but his cold departure in the morning.

Silence thrummed. Her lips were slightly parted and her eyes were on his. And he was so close to succumbing... But then he heard a low gecker from their audience on the fence, followed by a small coo. He glanced over her shoulder as three possibly wise monkeys brought him sharply to reason, and instead of kissing her and doing more, so much more, Carter used his mouth for good.

'Goodnight, Grace.'

He saw the dart of confusion in her eyes, the warmth of her cheek flaring to heat his palm as he denied them.

But surely it was better this way?

He was here to gather information and then get the hell out. He knew, too, that being here always put him in a dark place.

As well as that, she hadn't been versed in his cold and soul-less heart—those gorgeous green eyes were unaware that he had nothing, *nothing* other than sex to give.

'You should go in,' he said, dropping his hand and then watching as she fumbled in her small bag for her key.

Grace took two attempts to get the blasted key in the lock. Humiliated and embarrassed as the sexiest man she'd ever en-countered sent her off to bed without so much as a kiss when she'd been so sure.

With her back turned she bit her lip at the sting of his re-jection. But, used to hiding her true feelings, she managed an over-the-shoulder smile.

'Goodnight.'

'Sleep well.'

She closed the door between them and felt the breeze from the fan, but it neither cooled nor composed her.

She felt awkward and upset that she'd so spectacularly misread things. But as she stripped off her sarong and put out her clothes for the morning Grace groaned in embarrassment when she thought about how she'd shown him the elephant videos, then droned on about her mother.

God, no wonder she hadn't been on a date in for ever, or been kissed in…

Grace honestly couldn't remember.

Actually, she could. That guy at teaching college. But as she stepped into the shower his name remained elusive.

Carter wouldn't kiss like he had.

That much she knew.

Even the shower did little to smother the orchestra trapped in her frustrated body, for it played on tunelessly. Only now it played into a void. She shaved her legs—just because—and she shaved under her arms, conditioned her hair… But it was her centre that ached for attention. Her small breasts felt too big, and between her thighs she ached, even as she wrapped herself in a towel.

Of course he didn't want her in that way, Grace reprimanded her reflection in the mirror over the sink. He'd merely been passing the time.

Her cheeks were still flushed as she brushed her teeth— and, no, it wasn't from the wind on the boat or the sun. Replacing her toothbrush, she stared at her reflection in the dim low-wattage light and wished that Carter stood behind her and touched her cheek where he just had. Wished the night had ended differently.

As she lay in bed the monkeys scampered across the roof for a while, but soon even they gave in and she was left with a heavy regret.

She wished she'd known Carter Bennett's kiss.

Then, just on the edge of sleep, when her defences slipped a fraction, allowing her to wander the unguarded corridors in her mind, she dared admit to more.

She wished she'd known far more than just his kiss…

CHAPTER FOUR

THE NIGHTMARES WERE BACK.

Carter had considered them long since gone, but after more than two decades' absence they'd returned.

As always, they started benignly. He was casually strolling through Kuala Lumpur Airport, pulling up his boarding pass on his phone, when he heard his father's voice.

'Carter, look!'

Nonplussed, he turned and saw Grace, saw her passport lying on the floor.

Just like last time, he decided it wasn't his problem.

Damn.

There was a feeling of obligation he could not ignore.

'Grace!' he called out. 'Grace!' he said again, and then remembered she couldn't hear him.

Grace really *was* Sleeping Beauty now.

Instead of an airport bench she lay on a glass altar. There was no velvet rope parting them, nor a carpeted floor to cross, just dense jungle between them, and her passport was sinking into the swamp that surrounded her.

'Grace!'

He tried to call out to her again. Warn her that she'd never get home if she lost it. That she shouldn't be heading into the jungle in the first place. If she did…

Even in sleep, Carter did not allow himself to complete the thought.

Even in sleep, he refused to remember.

Instead he shot awake, as he'd trained himself to do decades ago, and snapped his eyes open.

Thankfully it took him less than a second to orientate himself—the dark wood, the high beams, and the background noise of a jungle that was never truly silent.

'Damn!'

He sat up and hauled himself out of bed, ruing his decision to return—especially by river.

Washing his face, he saw the shadows beneath his eyes and blamed them on the lack of sleep.

For once, it wasn't because of sex.

He'd wanted her badly, but he was a cold bastard at best.

And here he was at his worst.

So instead of bedding the gorgeous Grace he'd put that restless energy into something a little less destructive.

He'd told Jamal to go to bed and then had a few choice words with those movie executives…

He thought a swim might clear his head, so he went through his luggage and found running shorts his assistant would have packed and, having pulled them on, he grabbed a sarong and tied it on his hips.

His head was pounding, and not eased by the humid air as he stepped outside. Even the water was too warm as he dived in.

Morning hadn't even broken, yet the day already felt far too long.

Grace wasn't faring much better.

She was still cringing, of course, but Carter had told her he was leaving today, so hopefully she wouldn't have to face the man she'd…

She'd what? she challenged herself as she walked towards the jetty.

She hadn't dived into his arms or moved towards his mouth.

She'd just…

Hoped…

Thought that maybe…

'Morning!' Arif greeted her with a smile. 'Felicity will be with you soon. Oh, and there's a treat tonight,' he told her, and pointed to the sky. 'We'll be meeting a bit later. Felicity will give you the details.'

'Thanks.'

Then she saw Arif look over her shoulder.

'Hey,' he said, and a very fond smile lit his face. 'Finally!'

Grace knew that the person behind her had to be Carter.

'Arif,' he said.

And she stood there as he joined them, braced herself to come face to face with him, but was woefully unprepared. As he came into view the sight of him, dripping wet and wearing only a sarong tied low on his hips, was a lot to deal with at this hour.

She had to fight not to look at his body, to ignore the long, yet muscular arms and the fan of black hair on his chest.

'Morning.' Grace forced a pleasant smile, only it wavered when she saw his pallor and the dark rings under his eyes.

He looked grey compared to the way he'd looked last night. So much so that had Arif not been standing there she might even have forced her own awkwardness aside and asked if he was feeling all right. Then again, she doubted he'd have appreciated her concern, for her smile wasn't returned.

He just gave a vague nod, then addressed Arif. 'I'll get us both coffee…'

Grace felt her teeth grit at his cool dismissal and headed to the jetty.

'Here she is!' Felicity was clearly raring to go. 'Okay, that's everyone.'

As the boat pulled out she saw Carter and Arif were sitting opposite each other in the dining area, but quickly she looked away. It was their last morning boat trip. Tomorrow they were going on a jungle walk. And Grace didn't want to waste this gorgeous day…didn't want the highlight of her time here to be him.

As the boat made its lazy way along the river, the beauty of the new day greeted her. Herons skimmed the water, and the trees teemed with life, which at times they stopped to observe.

Watching the little silver leaf monkeys happily play— swinging, running along the branches and jumping—should make last night a little easier to forget.

And yet she kept remembering.

Little things…

The littlest of things…

How he'd looked—really looked—at her little video of the elephants. Told her how he'd once found a calf…

It hadn't seemed as if she was boring him then.

And he was the first person she'd ever told about her mother.

Well, aside from Violet, her awful cousin, Tanya, as well as the doctors, nurses and…

Carter was the first person she'd told not because it was necessary to do so, but because it was a huge part of her life…

'No luck!'

Felicity brought her back to the present. It would seem there would be no wild orangutans either.

'Just a nest,' Felicity added, putting down her binoculars and smiling at Grace. 'I know you've been itching to see one.'

'Not just one! I'd love to see a family,' Grace admitted.

'Oh, the males don't hang around after mating.' Felicity shook her head, and then punched her hand with her fist. 'Hit and run.'

Grace blinked. She'd heard the blunt terminology from Arif, but it sounded rather more shocking when delivered in Felicity's well-spoken voice. Then again, Felicity was a vet, and very earthy, and happily pointed out mating wildlife and so on. All the stuff that made Grace blush from her hair roots to her toenails when she thought about it…

It hadn't last night.

Grace screwed her eyes closed, determined not to be so pathetic. Only as they headed back for breakfast, instead of scanning the trees for signs of life, she was back to dreaming about Carter, barely noticing that the boat had slowed, as it often did when they passed longhouses.

'He's very well camouflaged...' Felicity told them, and Grace realised she must have spotted something as they drifted.

Hoping, *hoping*, that she was finally going to see an orang-utan in the wild, she was about to look up when she saw that Felicity was pointing downwards.

'How old...?' Randy asked as Corrin focussed her camera.

'Perhaps six months...less than a year...'

It was then that Grace saw the tiny crocodile, possibly the length of her forearm, his shiny skin yellow and brown, much like the muddy river bank, his little jaw wide open as he bathed in the morning sun.

He was cute, Grace thought, and attempted a joke. 'You know what *not* to do,' she said.

'What's that?' Felicity asked.

'Smile...'

Nobody got Grace's little joke about the old song warning people never to smile at crocodiles, so she sat there blushing as Felicity first of all blinked in bemusement and then addressed the group.

'Saltwater crocodiles are a huge problem for the locals. Their dogs and chickens are easy prey, but also small children, fishermen...'

'The Bennett family...' Randy drawled. 'Three killed...'

'Well, we don't think the crocodile directly killed all three,' Felicity said, in rapid defence of nature. 'It's believed that the father drowned trying to save his wife and baby boy...' She spoke on about the new hunting rules that were meant to deal with the threat. Then, 'That little fellow might look sweet, but he can grow to more than six feet in length and has a life-span of seventy years.'

'Bennett?' Grace checked—because wasn't that Carter's surname?

'Probably happened before your time,' Randy said, then looked to their guide. 'Is the Bennett place where you're based?'

'It is.' Felicity nodded.

Grace was trying to listen as Felicity explained about her grant, and her research, and how she was based at Wilbur Bennett's home, yet try as she might to concentrate, her mind kept drifting.

Was it Carter's family that had been killed?

Randy confirmed that it was. 'Saw him at the pool this morning—you should see the mess of his back.'

'That wasn't from the crocodile attack,' Felicity intervened, but to no avail.

'Shame he's going to turn it into a film set,' Randy said. 'Though you can't blame the guy for wanting nothing to do with the place.'

Felicity looked flustered, clearly trying to dampen the conversation down. 'That's just rumour and speculation…'

Things had moved *way* beyond rumour and speculation!

Arif had brought him up to speed.

'I didn't know whether to call,' Arif admitted. *Again.*

Carter didn't respond to those words, just poured another coffee as Arif spoke on.

'I wasn't sure you'd even want to know.'

'Well, I know now,' Carter retorted briskly. 'And I'm on to it.'

They had discussed the issue for a good couple of hours, and Arif seemed less than reassured by Carter's solutions.

'Barristers, lawyers, attorneys…' Arif gave a tight smile, clearly frustrated by the lack of direction and nervous about the path ahead. 'The damage is happening *now*. We've even got some of the executives staying here at the resort, although they didn't introduce themselves as such.'

'I saw.'

'They leave this morning, thank goodness. Though they prefer not to travel by river.' He stared back at Carter. 'They're flying in and out from *your* helipad.'

'Not this morning.'

'There's a boat booked to take them there; they have Benedict's permission.'

'Well, they don't have mine.' He told Arif what he'd done. 'I had words with them last night—told them in no uncertain terms that I was in residence and denied them all access.'

God, but he loathed this joint ownership. Carter abhorred anyone encroaching on his space at the best of times.

'I also made it clear that, whatever Benedict might have told them, I would not be selling.'

'Good.' Arif nodded, a touch mollified now.

Carter saw that the groups were starting to return from their trips and knew he and Arif were about to head to the office.

Or they should have been.

'Are you okay, Carter?' Arif checked.

'Of course.' He nodded, realising Arif had noticed his distraction.

He'd caught sight of Grace helping herself to breakfast.

She poured juice and selected fruit, and as she turned she looked over, just for a second, her lips parted as if she had a question. But then her mouth snapped closed and she turned her back.

Good, Carter thought. *Turn away now.*

He was leaving for his grandfather's residence after this day with Arif, and anyway she was by far too sweet for a jaded cynic like him...

Even though things between him and Arif were tense there was a moment of relief as they moved to the office. He heard

Arif let out a soft laugh at the sight of the executives mopping their brows as they climbed onto a boat to commence their long journey to the airport.

Carter barely noticed them. He could feel Grace's gaze on his back, on his scars, and though he was more than used to it, he felt an aching need to turn around.

Instead, he headed into the office with Arif and there stared at maps of the river he'd rather avoid. Heard about the programmes being run, and the disruption his cousin and his contacts were causing…

'Bornean banded pitta.' Arif tapped at the map for perhaps the fiftieth time, this time mentioning a rare bird. 'Abandoned three eggs…' he told Carter. 'And Felicity has data on the helmeted hornbill—so rare, but starting to return until the drones went up.' Arif spoke with both knowledge and passion. 'It's a declining species.'

It was late in the afternoon when Arif suggested that they walk.

Carter, though still only in his sarong, nodded. There needed to be no delay for getting changed—it made no difference here.

The grounds were extensive, with a boardwalk that skirted the jungle. And beyond were tens of thousands of hectares— a relative drop in the ocean, and yet untouched and vital and so full of life. And what he was here to discuss.

'How come you're still working as a guide?' Carter asked. 'I thought you'd be too busy co-ordinating all the projects.'

'I try to let the scientists do their work.' Arif shrugged. 'They don't need me looking over their shoulders. Anyway, I already know there are two new baby orangutans this month alone on your land.'

Carter thought of Grace and how she ached to see them in the wild—and, while this Felicity might be right about the jungle not being a zoo, he wished Grace could have seen them.

'Look…' Arif said, and lithely leapt over the wooden fencing. He glanced back, as if expecting Carter to follow, though he made no comment when he didn't.

Watching Arif disappear into the thick foliage, Carter felt a curl of dread, though he did his level best to ignore it. He stood scanning the trees, noting the freshly broken branches that had caught Arif's attention, and then exhaled in relief when Arif reappeared.

'Anything?' he asked.

'Pygmy elephant tracks. The groups saw them last night—that's why they were late back…'

'I heard.'

As they walked in silence, Carter again thought of Grace, and how last night he'd seen them through her eyes, as if for the first time. Her laughter and excitement, her sheer wonder, had brought some of the allure and the magic back.

If he could have made the journey here with his eyes closed he would have, or even kept them fixed ahead. Yet somehow Grace had forced them open, reminding him of better times…

'Do you remember when I thought I'd found that calf?' he said suddenly. 'I was so sure it was lost.'

Arif laughed. 'The herd was watching. The mother would not have been pleased if you'd approached him. She'd have attacked.'

It was the first real conversation they'd had about times prior to the incident…a time where they'd been just kids and friends…and Carter quickly regretted it—because Arif pounced.

'Do you ever think of going back into the jungle—to where it happened, to where you were found?' Arif asked, as he always did. 'My father is too old now, but I would come with you, of course. It's the anniversary soon—it might help you…'

'With what?' Carter challenged. 'I survived and I'm grateful. I've moved on with my life. I don't see the point of going there.'

As well as that, he did not need any reminder of the looming date.

They arrived back at the resort as dusk was falling. 'Stay for dinner,' Arif invited. 'It's the new moon, so we'll eat a bit later tonight, but we'd love you to join us.'

'I think it better that I head for the property,' Carter declined. 'I'll get straight on to Jonathon and tell him to progress things.'

He glanced around the resort and knew that his restless eyes were looking for Grace. Yes, it would be better by far to get the hell away.

'We'll catch up soon. I'll keep you informed.'

'I'll have your things moved to your boat...' Arif said, but then hesitated. 'First, though...' he nodded in the direction of his office '... I have something that is yours.'

Carter frowned.

'Give me a moment,' Arif said. 'I'll just ask Jamal to excuse us.'

Carter was not used to waiting outside anyone's office, but he stood there, no doubt about to be delivered another lecture and to be told he wasn't doing enough.

'Hey...'

He looked up and there was Grace, her hair wild and curly, her lemon top bright. Her face, which had been pale at the airport, now had a light dusting of freckles across her nose. Compared to last night, her eyes seemed a bit guarded, but her soft voice told him she was pleased that he was still here.

Walk away now, he wanted to warn her, because his black heart would soon darken those clear green eyes.

But instead of walking she stood there. 'I thought you'd gone,' she said.

'I'm about to.'

'Oh.'

She was waiting for him to elaborate, but deliberately he did not. His eyes had left her face, trying to ignore the soft curves of her slender body, how her yellow top, damp from the humid air, clung to her small breasts and narrow waist and skimmed her flat stomach. Despite the warmth her nipples were hard—not obviously so, unless you ached to know them, touch them, taste them…

Even looking down at her sneakers did not ease his sensual thoughts, for her legs were smooth and beneath those sneakers he knew there were coral-painted nails. It was her voice, though, the slight uncertainty to her tone that he deeply ached to address. Yes, he wanted to admit to her, she was right… this attraction was real.

His words might be curt, but physically he was lying. His body was beckoning hers, his arms were aching to draw her in. His stomach was tight, aching to fight arousal, yet his nonchalant stance, leaning on the wall, denied the untapped passion that thrummed between them.

'Well…' Grace said into the long silence. 'It was nice meeting you.'

He nodded.

'I'd better go and get ready for dinner…'

Carter frowned, looked at the darkening sky. He knew the routines here, and that a new moon meant dinner would be served later, but he did not want to get into conversation.

'Yep.'

He was abrupt in his dismissal, but better that she walked off a bit hurt and confused than that he take her by the hand and get her the hell out of here as he so badly wanted to.

'Arif is ready for you.' Jamal came then, and gave him a small, almost sympathetic smile. 'It's been nice seeing you, Carter.'

'Thank you.' He pulled himself away from the wall, barely glancing at Grace as he stepped into Arif's office, with no idea what was to come.

It was just a small workstation, really. A desk with pictures of the various guides on the walls, along with their beloved wildlife, as well as the usual office equipment.

Arif was standing behind his desk and he asked Carter to

close the door, then addressed him. 'You asked the point of going back to where it happened?'

'No,' Carter corrected. 'I said I see no purpose in *me* going back.'

'You anger is misdirected.'

'No.'

'Yes,' Arif insisted. 'How can you fight for something you don't love? You blame the land.'

'I don't.' Carter closed his eyes. He did not want a lecture, and while he admired Arif, while they might have once been close friends, Arif did not have any deep knowledge of him.

'You blame your parents, then?'

Carter stared ahead.

'Yourself?' Arif pushed, and their eyes met.

Carter's flashed a warning for Arif to leave things.

'I found this.'

Carter frowned when he saw Arif's eyes fill with tears.

'It is not mine to keep…'

He pushed a silk pouch forward on the desk and Carter glanced down. When he made no move to touch it, Arif opened the cord and slid a heavy band of solid silver onto the desk.

The walls seemed to fall, and the floor must have dissolved, for everything disappeared. And even though Carter didn't touch it, in one blinding flash he saw perhaps a hundred occasions when he'd picked up this silver teething ring and handed it to Hugo. Seen his brother's wide pink smile and that one tiny tooth, his little fat hand reaching out, clasping the ring and biting down on it.

His voice, when finally it came, was a raw husk. 'Where did you find this?'

'Close to where it happened.'

'But every inch was searched…' Carter argued the facts, but then halted, because that made him sound naive. Of course the jungle was not a neat field. 'When?'

'A year ago,' Arif said. 'Almost. I went back on the anniversary, I was placing offerings on behalf of your grandfather when I saw something glinting…'

Carter stared ahead rather than look down at the familiar silver as Arif spoke on.

'I remember you once asking your mother if it would break his teeth.'

Now he looked down at the teething ring…so familiar. It had first been his grandfather's, his father's, his, and then Hugo's. Polished to perfection for each new child.

The same had been done now. He could see Arif or Jamal must have spent hours lovingly making sure it gleamed.

And even though he still didn't touch it, there was no damage that he could see. Apart from a few tiny scratches, it might be sparkling in the finest antique jeweller's.

He wished he could pick it up, hold it, trace the little scratches on the silver that Hugo's one little tooth had made. But he would not stand in an office and weep as expected. He did not know how to summon emotion on demand—for he'd rather have none.

'I know you must—' Arif started, but Carter stopped him right there.

'You have no idea how I feel.'

'That's just it—you refuse to feel!' Arif said.

He was perhaps the only person on the planet who would speak so bluntly to Carter, but they had known each other since they were both still called Ulat. They had spent summers together before tragedy had struck as well as after.

Arif picked up the teething ring and held it out to him. 'You won't even touch it?'

'You should have left it there…'

'Why?'

'Because that's where it belongs. With him. Undisturbed.' Carter was not a suspicious person, but in this he was certain. 'I think it should be returned.'

'That is for you to decide.'

'On the anniversary,' Carter nodded, relieved it was about to be sorted, but Arif had misunderstood what he meant.

'I have a conference on the exact date, but if you want me to take you in, then I shall cancel it.'

'I meant for you to return it.'

'No.' Arif shook his head. 'It is your property.'

Carter watched as he returned the teething ring to the pouch.

'I shall have it packed along with your things.'

'Fine.' Carter refused to plead, and just stared at Arif. 'I'll be in touch.'

He walked out, refusing to look back, ready to board his boat and get away. But he had to wait for his things, and as well as that he needed to breathe before facing that journey.

Damn you, Arif...

He strode past the deserted dining room and out to the boardwalk, then leant against the wooden rail and stared up at the dark near-moonless sky. He did not want to be here. God knew if Benedict turned up now then he'd be tempted to just sign over the place if it meant he could get the hell out...

Then he heard a sharp, panicked intake of breath and, turning around, realised it was Grace walking towards him and that he'd scared her.

'It's just me.'

Grace put her hand to her chest and exhaled in relief, but her heart was still hammering.

'What are you doing out here?' he asked.

She shrugged and went to walk on, still hurt by his dismissal, but she didn't want to look churlish. 'I messed up with the tour,' Grace admitted. 'I knew the times had changed tonight, but I thought dinner was before we went out.'

'It's a new moon,' he explained.

She frowned, not understanding.

'Didn't Felicity tell you?'

'Probably,' Grace said. 'I wasn't really listening.'

She certainly wasn't about to admit she'd spent most of today trying not to think about him.

Now, standing in the oppressive, humid air, she saw the tension on his features.

Heard his silence.

'I'll leave you in peace.' She started to walk off.

'There's no peace to be had here.'

Grace paused and, given what she'd found out today, she understood why he felt that way.

'Someone on the tour said something about...' She took a breath and made herself ask. 'Was it your family who were attacked?'

'Yes.'

'I'm so sorry.'

'It was a very long time ago.'

'Even so...' It was too dark to read his features, but he must have seen her eyes move to his scar. 'Felicity said...'

'There are a lot of rumours. None of them true. I was there, and even I don't know what happened.'

She waited, but he didn't elaborate or tell her what that meant.

Even the thought of him having been there made her shiver. She doubted he'd appreciate knowing that, so she quickly blamed her shudder on the dark night.

'I feel as if a hundred pairs of eyes are watching me.'

'Thousands,' he corrected.

'Don't.' She gave a nervous laugh. 'Really?'

'Of course.'

There was the sudden hoot of an owl and a rustle of the low bushes nearby and she moved a little closer to the other human present. Only the other human present startled her more than the jungle at night, because he placed a hand on her bare arm and the contact was electric.

* * *

'It's fine,' he told her, when there was a loud crash in the trees behind them. 'It's just your friends the elephants.'

'How do you know?'

'I used to…' He halted. 'I used to know these things.'

They looked out into the night and listened for several moments. The silence between them was far gentler now, and his eyes were narrow, yet alert, as the noise faded into the distance.

'Aren't they too close?' Grace asked. 'I mean…' She looked at the wooden fence that lined the boardwalk.

'It's their land,' Carter said, and they both turned to lean on the fence. 'The staff are all aware. If they get too close they'll try to move them back. They're quite a way away.'

He looked at her properly then. She was wearing her sarong, and it was the first time he'd seen her with her hair down. He knew he'd hurt her, and it pricked his conscience.

'I was short with you before,' he said. 'I apologise.'

'It's fine.'

'No.' He shook his head. 'You didn't deserve it.'

Now it was Grace who turned and looked at him.

'I can see why you don't care what happens to your grandfather's home, but…' She swallowed. 'It's just sad to think of it changing.'

'What did you hear?' he asked, then guided her so that she stood in front of him.

He moved her so easily, Grace thought, and she went so easily. It was as if the wooden floor beneath her feet was air, or she was skating on ice.

Not that she'd ever skated. But even so the thought made her smile as she faced him—or was it the simple relief that they were talking again and alone? His scent cut through the dank humid air, and they were staring at each other as intently as they had the moment they met.

'What's everyone saying?' he asked.

'That you're going to have a film crew come here.' She looked for a reaction but got none. 'It would be a shame to spoil it.'

'Arif would concur.'

She must have heard the edge to his voice. 'Did you two just have an argument?'

'I guess you could call it that.'

Carter didn't tell her what it had been about, though, and nor did he tell her the plans were his cousin's, deciding that in this case perhaps it was better the devil she *didn't* know. A sell-out and a power-hungry rat she would possibly be able to fathom more easily than a man whose heart had turned to stone at the age of eight. A man who was a cold, empty shell, who could crush a pretty soul like Grace's in the palm of his hand.

Yet she stood as if undaunted—in fact she disputed the supposed evidence.

'It's just rumours,' she added.

And in her sarong her shoulders were near naked, her dark curls were still wet from the shower, and he didn't care about the rules tonight.

'I missed you last night,' he told her.

She let out a short, incredulous breath, minty and fresh, and he looked down at the mouth he had forced himself to deny.

He could deny it no more.

Grace found out not only what she'd missed last night, but all she'd been missing. For when his mouth lightly grazed hers, she almost folded inside at the slow, sensual contact.

He could have kissed her the moment she met him, Grace now knew, as her lips brushed his, parting a little. It might have been described as a light kiss, but it was potent, for no contact was broken and she closed her eyes to the heady bliss.

As his hand slid to her waist he pulled her into him. The

slip of his tongue, her involuntary moan, seemed to inflame him, as if he'd been waiting for this kiss for a very long time.

So, too, had she.

His kiss was masterful, honed to perfection, and when she closed her eyes, when she sank into sheer bliss, Grace didn't even care how those skills had been acquired, she just relished their application.

He tasted her, curled her tongue, sucked the tip, so slow and thorough. And that combined with the expensive scent of him, and the heat from his naked torso, had her coveting more of him. She pressed her hands on his bare chest—not to push him away, just to feel beneath, to touch him and feel the fan of hair—then moved them up to his hair, simply to feel more of him.

There was no comparison to the teenage kisses she'd known. It felt like a discovery as she simply allowed the passion in. His hands were more specific—one came to her breast and felt it through the flimsy fabric. She should remove his hand, Grace knew, tell him it was too much, too soon. Only it wasn't enough, and it was by far too late, for she'd ached for this since last night.

She felt her stomach tense low down as he lifted her hair and kissed her neck with the same deep attention he had given her mouth. His hand left her breast and pulled her closer in, and possibly he lifted her a little, for her bare feet felt as if there was no ground beneath them.

Her eyes were closed, her mouth frantic. 'Why didn't you kiss me last night?' she breathed.

'Shh…' he said, kissing down her neck towards her shoulder. 'I'm kissing you now…'

'Why?' she asked again, still bemused, only more so now. A night and a day of frustration had her demanding answers and she moved her neck so they faced each other, breathless, mid-kiss, suspended in want. She could feel where his mouth had been, and watched as he pondered her question.

'Because you don't know me.'

'You don't know me either, Carter,' she responded. Because if he knew she had never been touched, or the true chaos of her life back home, then she was certain he'd be gone.

'If you did know me, you'd know we can go nowhere. I don't do relationships.'

'So, you think with one kiss I'd assume we were in a relationship?'

'Grace, I think we both want more than one kiss.'

She swallowed, more than aware of her own desire. Certainly she could feel his, wedged against her stomach, beguiling and tempting.

'As I said, you don't know me. I don't get involved.'

But, again, Carter didn't know her either.

They really were going nowhere.

In a few weeks she'd be back home, facing the problems she'd left behind, and right now she felt this rare liberty—as if this was the only real chance she had to be free, to know herself, to be with another person as the woman she wanted to be.

She knew, too, as she had on sight, that she did not belong in Carter's world, and nor did he belong in hers.

They met tonight, in this rare, sultry place, and for the first time in so many years she wasn't scared about tomorrow.

'Yes.' Grace nodded. 'I do want more than a kiss.'

He slid his hands down her hips, held her bottom, while his eyes never left her face.

'We can go back to my grandfather's place,' Carter said, then added, 'Take my boat.'

She pulled her head back. 'I thought...' She swallowed. 'Can't we go to your suite?'

'Here?' He frowned taking her face in his hands, looking right into her eyes.

'Please.'

'Are you a quiet lover?' he asked, and she felt her cheeks burn beneath his palms.

'I don't know,' Grace responded. 'Maybe?'

It was the closest she could come to telling him she'd never made love.

CHAPTER FIVE

CARTER STEPPED INTO a speedboat and then offered her his hand.

Grace took it gladly.

She knew there was no future, no romance. Just this night…

And she knew she might never again get the chance to be wild and free and with someone so beautiful.

After six missing years Carter made her brave enough to discover this side of herself.

His speedboat was beautiful, with a small cabin and plush, comfortable seats, and instead of releasing her after she'd boarded he pulled her in and kissed her again. A soft, slow kiss that told her this was all okay.

'It's an hour or so, with a stop on the way—and, yes,' he said, as he started the engine. 'I'll get you back for your dawn—'

'Actually,' Grace cut in, 'there's no dawn tour. Tomorrow it's a jungle walk…'

Carter felt his chin rise, his shoulders and neck tightening—though it was not echoes of the past that had tension ripping through him, but thoughts of her in the jungle tomorrow.

'Who's…?' Even his vocal cords had tightened, and he cleared his throat as the boat moved off. 'Is Arif taking the group out?'

'No, I think it's Felicity.'

He said nothing, his eyes fixed ahead. He'd barely heard of Felicity, let alone seen her, but knew she wasn't a local and was here doing research. He reminded himself that Arif wouldn't let her take a group out if she wasn't skilled, but hadn't Felicity been here mere months?

It was dark, with no glint of moon, and even the stars were hidden behind low black clouds as they put-putted past the longhouses. But when they turned off the main river…when the last of the light was gone…he heard her deep intake of breath…

'You're fine,' he said, drawing her close so she stood by him.

'Will we see other boats?'

'Most can't get down here,' Carter said, and steered them into a small tributary, then another, where the branches were hanging low, the banks closer, forming a natural tunnel. He guided them down, then they came to some mangroves and he turned the engine off.

'What are you doing?' she whispered as he turned the lights off and they were plunged into darkness.

He turned her around and wrapped his arms over her shoulders. 'Look,' he told her.

'I can't see anyth—'

For a second she thought she had something in her eye. Little lights were darting across her vision. But then she gasped as she saw the river trees as if draped in fairy lights, flickering on and off, dots of yellow and cool icy green.

'Fireflies,' she gasped.

'And a new moon,' he said. 'Which makes them especially bright. Now do you get why the group went out later tonight?'

Grace started to laugh—a giddy laugh, a carefree laugh—and she spun around, stunned by the tiny lights, the sheer volume of them.

'It looks as if they've been strung on the branches…as if…' She had never seen anything so beautiful, so pretty, so wondrous. Some of the lights darted, and some of them seemed to flash in unison, as if synchronised. 'This is so precious!'

'Yes.' He turned her to face him. 'And so are you,' he stated, for he needed her so badly tonight.

Beyond the display in the lush trees where the fireflies gathered were the bare, silvery mangroves where his family had been lost. Where not only his heart had been carved out but his spirt, too, leaving him a stranger to those who had once known him.

'Take another look,' he said. 'They disappear once the lights come on.'

For Grace, they would never disappear.

Even before they'd made love the night was perfect. As if Carter himself had been standing on ladders and arranging the lights just to give her this sight.

'Thank you,' she said as he started up the boat. The light show was over but her heart was soaring even as they were plunged back into the night. Bolder now, she moved behind him as he took the wheel. Wrapping her arms around his waist she leant her head on his strong back and gazed out to the darkness. 'For bringing me here.'

Carter loathed the rare times he was here. It was like sailing through hell. But tonight he felt the low grip of her arms around his waist as he stared ahead. Feeling her warmth, he carefully guided the boat through the winding, narrow stretch. The dense vegetation was gone; the river here was lined on either side with bare silvery mangroves.

Grace's touch, the heat from her body and the promise of bed was everything he needed to get through this stretch of river he particularly loathed.

'Was it here?' she asked, and he assumed she must have felt the tension zip through his shoulders.

Usually he'd ignore such a question, but then, there was nothing usual about this situation. He'd avoided being here, and certainly had never brought a woman. There was no demand for him to answer…just a calm, patient presence…and they were, after all, just together for one night.

'Just there,' he finally answered, pointing to the exact spot. 'That was where my father tied the boat off. A local fisherman saw it empty.'

He turned the boat's flashlight on and aimed it towards the riverbank, but there were no predatory glinting eyes, just the pale mangroves and the still, dark water. He thought of his mother, impatient when they couldn't get the small boat close enough…

'Sophie!'

He could almost hear his father warning her…see Hugo smiling over her shoulder, looking at him.

Moving the flashlight, he shone it into the mangroves, almost expecting to see Hugo's innocent smile.

That damn teething ring.

Arif should have left it there, undisturbed.

Carter turned off the flashlight, and Grace knew he was shutting down any further discussion about it. She didn't blame him.

It was eerie to be on the river now, a relief to leave that stretch behind.

More so for Carter.

'Not long,' he said, as they turned down another waterway and finally she glimpsed lights.

'Are there people at home?' she asked as he tied the boat.

'There are some residences and offices, but their jetty is further along.' She saw him look at her taut features. 'Don't worry, Felicity won't see us. The banyan tree is a great divider.'

She laughed. 'Why am I so scared of her?'

'I don't know.' He pointed to his laptop and she passed it out to him. 'That too,' he said, and she handed him the leather cylinder he'd been carrying at the airport.

'So much for spontaneous,' she quipped.

'When it rains in Borneo…' he said, offering his hand and pulling her out. 'I am not risking them.'

The lawn was so unlike the jungle, trimmed and cold beneath her feet, and then they came to a stone path and walked up some steps.

'Wait here…' he told her, and she watched as he opened up some French doors.

She gasped as he turned on lights. 'A ballroom?'

'It was,' he said. 'Now it's a conference room, but there used to be parties held here. Arif and I would watch.'

He didn't elaborate, just deposited his luggage by the doors and then his attention was fully upon her.

She felt shy, and just a touch awkward—possibly because of her inexperience, or just because she was here, in this stunning, opulent home, where apparently you entered via a ballroom.

But then she met his eyes and any gathering doubts flew away. For there was nothing in her head other than his male beauty. Not a thought save for one—that it *had* to be him. This night could only happen with him. On this hot, sultry island, all her secrets would be held in the jungle…a place she was never going to return.

'Can we dance?' she asked.

'I don't dance.'

'One dance,' she said, and draped her arms around his neck.

They swayed to no music and she inhaled the scent of his chest and then kissed his salty skin. Breathing him, licking him, tasting him… And not caring, barely noticing, when he unknotted her sarong and it fell to the polished wooden floor.

Oh, the feel of her breasts against his chest, his hands easing her knickers past her thighs. She pushed them down and stepped out of them.

'One more dance,' said the man who never danced as he discarded his clothing.

And she thought there might just be music, because they moved slowly as if to a rhythm.

His breathing was ragged in her ear, and then he took her hand and slipped it between them, and she held him, stroked him. Then they separated and he toyed with her breasts, lowering his head and tasting them one by one.

'Please...' she said when he stopped his attention there.

But he desisted, and neither did he pull her back into his embrace. The sight of the silver he'd left on her stomach was the most erotic thing she'd ever seen. His erection was alive between them, as if searching for where Grace ached the most.

'Take me to bed,' she pleaded, and he did.

But first—hopelessly unromantic—he took condoms from his luggage.

'I don't bring anyone here,' he told her.

She liked that. Knew this was a rarity for them both.

As he picked her up she coiled her legs around his waist. He took the long, winding grand stairs and kissed her at the top, then carried her down a corridor, then another...

She clung on to his neck, kissing his face, his mouth, his neck, feeling the passion she hadn't known she was capable of, or had simply not allowed to emerge.

Carter loathed coming here.

Past the photos...up the stairs.

The bombardment of memories felt too much at times, but tonight all he had to deal with was her body, coiled around him, and the kisses she rained on his face. Transported by desire, he opened the door to his wing and kissed her hard against the wall. His hand reached down. He was desperate to have her...the bedroom was by far too far away...

'Bed,' she insisted.

He kissed her all the way there then dropped her onto the bed, put the condoms aside, wanting first to taste her, and for her to put her mouth on him. He looked at her glittering eyes, her pale body, and then to her lips, wet from his kisses. He slid a hand between her thighs and felt her, warm and slick. He touched her tender spot and watched her bite her lip. He stroked her with light beats of pressure, watching her twitch, her knees lifting and her hand coming over his.

'Oh, God…' she gasped, and he forgot about mouths… forgot everything… For even though he wanted so badly to watch her come, he needed her more.

His kiss was fierce and consuming as he settled his thighs between her own, and he lifted and held himself, guided himself to her entrance.

He could feel her, slick and warm, and he heard her soft moans. She was so oiled he was tempted to simply slip in, to lose himself, but he hauled himself back from the edge and reached to the bedside.

Grace breathed in relief. The slight nudge of him had hurt and she wanted to regroup, to tell herself that it was done, he'd broken her, and he never had to know.

Her hand slid from his shoulder as he moved to get protection, and then she felt the waxy skin, the pitted cool flesh, and the thought of her own imminent pain receded.

She felt him still…felt as if she was touching something forbidden—as if beneath her fingers was a secret. She felt a crevice, felt the thick scar tissue beneath. She almost expected him to object by moving away, but he was still. She would never know him after this night, and she wanted to know what she could. So she continued to touch him, to feel the cool, tough flesh and the dints. She knew from his breathing that he was more than aware of her perusal, more intimate than her touch in the ballroom.

He was so aware. He felt her exploration. The skin on his back was usually dull to sensation, but always he was aware of a lover's recoil—as if they could not stand the imperfection, the truth that their polished lover was flawed.

Yet Grace's fingers felt like a gentle enquiry, and he closed his eyes at the tenderness of her touch, grateful for her lack of questions, her quiet acceptance.

Protection forgotten, he moved to enter her.

His kiss was deep and wet—a hungry kiss, a devouring kiss. His hand was on her cheek and there was an unvoiced concurrence as still she explored his naked back, moving down past his shoulders, low on his ribcage.

This was no accidental graze of her fingers. They stroked the damaged flesh and he did not know why he allowed it— just knew that here, in this hellhole he'd returned to, it helped.

He guided himself to ease inside her, and there was that resistance again—not her…he could feel her wanting and her softly parted thighs, the ache of desire cording them.

Then he met her eyes, like that very first time, and they were as clear and as perfect as they'd been when they'd first looked into his.

She confirmed what he'd just found out.

'I've never made love…'

'I don't do love,' he responded.

'I've never had sex.'

He stared down at her, wondering why a beautiful twenty-five-year-old might avoid such a vital pleasure?

They both had scars, Carter realised, and neither of them was denying them tonight.

'Do you want…?'

His voice was a low burr. He was trying to get his head around what he was being told, trying to claw for his usual logic, but she was almost sobbing, pleading…

'You know that I do.'

He had never made love to a virgin. There was no place in his bed for tender hearts. And yet those rules seemed to have vanished, and raw desire, older than the land that surrounded them, was calling. More than that, he wanted her untutored, untouched body, and as she closed her eyes he held his unsheathed, thick length and watched the grit of her teeth as he nudged in. He heard her moan and watched a tear squeeze from her closed eyes, and then he felt the tightness, and had to stop himself from sinking too fast into her exquisite pleasure.

'Look at me…' he told her.

She didn't know how to. But the searing agony was fading, and it was the most deeply intimate moment of her life—not just in the physical sense. His warm breath and his mouth were still above her, and his precision hadn't wavered when she'd revealed her truth.

So she looked at him, and for a moment there wasn't a single lie, nothing between them—just this night.

Then he closed his eyes and drove deeply in.

It hurt, but he pushed fully in, and although it hurt some more there was a giddy rush, a sense of liberty, a pure and intense pleasure, and she opened her eyes and stared back at him. She felt as if something had just been put right…as if this very moment was the reason she was here.

'No one ever has to know,' she whispered, liking the secret between them that here, for tonight, she could find herself.

She shuddered with pain and pleasure as he moved. The rawness and the sensations were too much, while conversely not enough, and when he drove in again she moaned, not wholly in pleasure.

He pushed her damp hair from her face and the slightly sick feeling receded. She had nothing with which to compare—just this deep sense that it could only ever have been him, because her body was coming alive, thrumming beneath him.

She had never locked eyes so intensely with another.

'Move with me,' he encouraged her, putting a hand on her bottom and lifting her as he drove more deeply in, then moving it to the small of her back as she moved of her own will to meet him.

'I'm going to come...'

'No,' he told her, because she wasn't lost yet.

He was deep in her tight space, so close to coming himself, and yet prolonging the intense pleasure by moving slower than his urgent desire.

He felt her holding on, hot and crying, watched her biting her lip. And he adored her internal fight, and the little pulses when she gave in. How she closed her eyes as she gripped him intimately.

He moved up onto his forearms and he took her, each thrust a little closer to the tempo he wanted to be met. He watched her eyes widen, felt her calves wrap around him, and there was something a little selfish about the way he took her, and something a little greedy about how she begged him.

Grace was sobbing and moaning in pleasure, her fingers digging into his taut buttocks, jolting with the raw power of him. She'd thought tonight she'd know pleasure—she'd never thought it would be so raw and pure.

Then he stilled and she felt a final swell. His shout was silent, and she felt as if her heart had been rapidly drained... as if every drop of life force had flooded her sex. And, no, she wasn't a noisy lover. She was almost as silent as him as the world went black and he spilled inside her. She felt tender, raw and exquisite with the depth of her orgasm and the intensity of his.

She knew she was crying...knew he was watching her fall apart beneath him, witnessing her unravel as she had never felt able to before.

She wanted to roll over, to curl up and hold her aching self, will herself back to calm. But she was on her elbows, watching his taut, flat stomach as he slowly slid out. And it was his hand that calmed her, grounded her as she tried to catch her breath.

When she rolled over it was not to turn away, but to turn in to him, her leg over his, his hand on her hip, her face, now burning from exertion and crying tears on his chest.

Then she watched a little fascinated as he positioned himself so that what had been hard inside her now lay long on his thigh. She could hear the hammer of his heart slowing, and guessed there were questions ahead, but then he kissed the top of her head, as if in a little sign of no regret.

And, for now, tomorrow just didn't matter.

CHAPTER SIX

CARTER BENNETT HAD been completely certain it would never happen to him.

So certain that he would only ever practise safe sex that he'd never got around to having the vasectomy he'd intended to.

He'd definitely never brought a woman back here—and nor did he generally lie in bed holding her after. But they were both silent, as if processing what had taken place, with Grace's head on his chest as he stared at the ceiling.

It was she who spoke first.

'You think I should have told you?'

He shook his head, but she was staring out of the French windows to the black moonless night so probably didn't see. 'You did tell me.'

'I meant earlier…' she amended. 'If I'd told you I was a virgin you'd have turned that speedboat around.'

Carter thought of how badly he'd needed her and wasn't so certain he would have.

'I didn't want your judgement,' Grace told him.

'What does that mean?'

'For you to assume I couldn't handle a one-night stand.' Her voice was defiant as she pulled away from his embrace and rolled onto her back, then pulled the sheet up to cover her. 'I put my life on hold for a long time. I'll no doubt be doing the same again in the near future.' She let out a shaky breath. 'I wanted a night like this before I went back to reality.'

'The reality is, we didn't use anything.'

The defiance left Grace. 'No...'

'You're not on the pill?'

'I'm not.'

She closed her eyes, knew that in that part she'd been way more reckless than planned.

'There's a pill for the morning after...' Even as she said it her voice trailed off. She was not sure if she wanted that option...

'I'll go to the pharmacy at nine,' he said.

Grace said nothing.

'That was a joke,' Carter said. 'Albeit a bad one...'

She turned, and was surprised to see that his rather haughty face wasn't accusatory—in fact his features were softened by the slightest smile.

'Grace, we are in the middle of nowhere.'

'True...' She found herself able to stay facing him. 'I wasn't thinking.'

'Neither of us were,' Carter agreed. 'And you're wrong. Had you told me back on the boat, I don't think I'd have turned around.' He paused, as if surprised by his own admission, but then he was frank. 'I would, however, have made it far clearer that we had no future. I don't get involved—'

Grace interrupted him. 'Carter, we have no future.' She looked him right in the eyes as she continued. 'That was the best part about it.'

She had no real future.

Not one that involved dating and romance. Instead she had a sick mother to support—what guy would understand that?

And until tonight she'd had no real past—not when it came to men.

Or dating.

No social life or adventures to count.

For years she'd lived in some sort of vacuum, focussing on taking care of her mother, working while she could, losing herself a little more each day. If it hadn't been for Violet, she'd barely have glimpsed the outside world.

'It was just tonight—and, believe me, that's all I wanted.'

'Why wait, though?' He frowned.

'I've had a lot going on. It kind of killed any chance of romance.'

'Well, if that's what you feel you've missed out on, then we are certainly missuited—because I don't do romance in any way shape or form.'

'I know,' Grace said, though she didn't necessarily agree.

She thought about the fireflies, the way he had held her, the dancing in the ballroom. Not to mention the fact that they were still in his gorgeous bed, talking. This felt more romantic than she'd ever hoped.

Still, rather than admit that, she tried to make a joke. 'At least I know now that I'm quiet in bed.'

He said nothing to that—didn't even smile.

Oh, why did her jokes always fall flat? Grace thought.

But then she felt a shift, so subtle it was nothing she could define...just a light tension between them.

And she knew it was the stir of arousal.

How, when she was still coming down from her first time?

She took a breath, trying to ignore his naked body lying beside her, trying to ignore the thrum in hers. Forcing herself to consider the ramifications of that one, heady indulgence.

'What if I am...?' She could barely say the word, the thought too daunting to contemplate.

'It will be dealt with.'

'Hmm...' Grace wasn't sure she wanted to know what his method of *dealing* with things might be.

'When are you due?'

When she didn't answer, he persisted.

'Grace, when was your last period?'

'I'm not sure…' She sat up, tried to get her head around dates, but it was hard to get her thoughts out of this night, let alone cast her mind back. 'Just before I came away.'

'It will most likely be okay.'

'Yep.' She took a breath and looked around the vast room. She knew he was trying to reassure her, but she didn't feel reassured. She'd always wondered how people lost their heads and took risks…in truth she'd privately been a bit dismissive…

Now she knew better.

'I ought to get back.'

'Already?'

She nodded, and went to get up, but he reached for her shoulder to halt her.

'Why are you being so brittle?'

'Because I feel stupid,' she admitted. 'Because I wanted everything that happened tonight, except for the part where we didn't use protection.' She ran a hand through her wild hair and refused to let him see how panicked she felt. 'Can I use your shower?'

'Of course.'

She glanced around the room for her clothes…

'They're in the ballroom,' he said.

'God, so they are.' She closed her eyes, a little mortified by the rather loose behaviour he seemed to have unearthed, but then opened them to his lazy smile.

'I'll find you a sarong.'

'Thank you.'

'I don't have any female underwear, though.'

'No hidden stash?' she teased, and instantly regretted it.

Except he laughed, and she could, right there, have gone over and kissed him. Finally, someone who got her stupid jokes.

She looked at him, lying with the sheet barely covering that gorgeous body that had been over hers, and deep inside.

* * *

'Shower?' Grace said.

'Just through there.' Carter pointed, watching as she climbed out of bed, seeing a little of the evidence on her thigh and her gorgeous bottom and hardening again.

'Can I use…?' she began.

She was as turned on as he, he could see the glitter in her eyes, the way she bit her lip, her thighs poised as if she might dive back into bed.

'Shampoo?'

'Sure.'

He was still pointing as she disappeared into the bathroom and Carter stared at his own finger and knew he'd been tempted to crook it…to beckon her back to bed.

And that was not him.

Oh, Carter partook in a lot of morning-after sex, but he viewed that as necessary…a little like brushing your teeth. You felt better for the rest of the day for having done it.

He wasn't so used to straight-after-sex sex, though…or resisting joining a lover in the shower.

He'd also like to correct her. He was rather certain she could soon be a very noisy lover.

And she was funny—that was new—lying in bed dwelling on another…

He liked her company and that was a whole other type of new.

Climbing out of bed, he picked up a couple of sarongs from his dresser. Covering the evidence of their coupling with the sheet, he left one out for the prior virgin, the other he wrapped around his hips, then walked out through the French doors and onto the balcony.

The sky was still navy, the dawn inching towards breaking. The clouds had drifted away, and the stars were taking their final moments to shine in the moonless sky. The usually muggy air had a morning-fresh tinge.

The recklessness of the night was concerning, but for now, very deliberately, he dwelt on the actual reason he was here.

He had dreaded returning, but it had been made easier by Grace.

This whole situation would be made easier by Grace.

He was certain she needed money for her mother, and he found it endearing that she refused to say.

God knew, he wasn't used to that.

He admired that she had come to his bed with purpose, wanting to lose her virginity. Hell, he completely got that a night that could go nowhere held appeal.

Certainly it had for him, on too many occasions.

And he knew that if there was such a thing here Grace Andrews would already have called for a taxi.

As for pregnancy…?

He closed his eyes. He would not cloud his thoughts with that.

For Carter that was a separate issue entirely.

It wasn't concern about a pregnancy, or a sense of charity, nor guilt that she'd been a virgin that had him considering his options. If he wanted to stop his cousin in his poisonous tracks, then marriage for a year would take care of that.

A year, though?

It had seemed unfathomable—in truth it still did. Yet for the first time he dwelt on that clause he'd so summarily dismissed.

Now it seemed doable.

He'd have to tell Grace why, though—have to share his past when he preferred not to. And he'd have to tell her that this place, even though he'd prefer that it didn't, still mattered to him.

'Hey…'

He turned his head as she came out on the balcony and joined him. Her hair was combed and slicked back.

'Thanks for this,' she said, gesturing to the black sarong he'd left out, then she looked up. 'Wow…' she said, gazing up at the canopy of stars and then staring down to the dark of the thick jungle stretched out in the distance. 'Which way is the resort?' she asked and her eyes followed to where he pointed. 'So, no chance of walking back?'

'None,' Carter agreed. 'Do you want breakfast?' he offered. 'We could take it up here and watch the sunrise. It's pretty incredible.'

He saw her hesitation, knew she really just wanted one night, and it actually strengthened him, made the thoughts in his head take clearer shape. He wanted to be certain before he voiced them.

'Are you going to cook?'

'I don't cook.' He wasn't going to summon breakfast, though. He didn't want anyone else invading, nor his thoughts interrupted. 'But Malay will have it all prepared in the kitchen. We can load up a tray and bring it back.'

'Sounds good.'

They walked through the house she had barely noticed last night, down the curved stairs, and she paused at a photo of a baby smiling.

'Is this your brother?' She looked at the gorgeous almond eyes and spiky hair, the wide smile.

'Why do you think that?' Carter asked.

'Well, he's blond, and far too smiley to be you.'

Carter gave a low laugh. 'You're wrong—that *is* me.'

They wandered down a little further, and they came to an image that had her throat squeezing tight.

His mother was too beautiful for words, with blonde hair and fine features. His father was handsome, but perhaps not as arrogant-looking as Carter. And there he was, smiling again.

Then she looked at the baby Carter held in his arms.

'He's blond too,' Grace said, and then wondered if she should have said *was*.

But all she could see was his soft spiky blond hair and huge eyes. He was such a beautiful baby, and his smile was so infectious that even though she felt her throat grow tighter she found that she was returning it.

Carter could not.

He didn't see the smile. He just stared. Not at his parents, nor at Hugo, but at the silver teething ring his brother held in his hand.

What the hell had Arif been thinking? He should have left it where it belonged.

He walked away, and Grace followed him into the gorgeous kitchen. It was old but very, very beautiful, and as he put some coffee on she took a high stool.

He wondered how to broach things.

How to explain that he was considering asking her to be his temporary wife.

'It looks as if you were a very happy family.' Grace was undoubtedly still thinking of the photos. 'Your parents were clearly in love.'

'It's easy to be happy when you don't have responsibilities,' Carter said dismissively. 'They were happy at the expense of others…' He glanced over. 'I find love to be selfish.'

'Selfish?' Grace checked, and he nodded.

'Extremely. My parents wanted adventure, to travel. To see the Northern Lights, sleep under the stars, trek through the jungle…'

'I think that's lovely.'

'Until it isn't. They had children.'

It had been Carter who had given Hugo his bottle when they'd gone out to gaze at a full moon. Carter who had checked there were enough provisions when they'd set out on yet another adventure.

While waiting for the coffee to brew he loaded a tray with a bowl of fruit and some pastries, and took some jugs from the fridge, scooping out some shaved ice.

'What are you making?'

'ABC,' he told her. *'Air batu campur,'* he explained, adding little balls of pale pink jelly to a bowl. 'Well, the cheat's version. Malay has made it—you just add your own fruit…'

And nuts, Grace thought, then tried to not pull a face when she saw him add to the tray a small dish of creamed corn. 'It looks more like a dessert.'

'Maybe…' In truth, he was unsure whether it was because of his mother's somewhat lackadaisical ways that Malay always served it for breakfast, or simply down to the heat.

There was too much he didn't know, and too many memories. As he walked down the corridor, past the framed photos, he deliberately didn't pause to look at them. He didn't need them, for there were new images dancing before his eyes: a flash of himself feeding Hugo spoonsful of ice-cream.

He was certain now that it was seeing the teething ring that was to blame for this surge in sensation. Arif might just as well have unearthed Carter's deeply buried heart.

There was a deep purple hue to the sky as they set up on the balcony, and he filled two bowls with ice, added the little balls of rosewater jelly and topped them with a red bean ice-cream.

'Choose your fruit…' he said, selecting some berries for himself.

She picked up a dark, heavy fruit, like a cross between a pomegranate and plum, but then, clearly unsure what to do with it, put it back.

Carter hesitated before reaching out for it. 'Give it here…'

She handed him the fruit she'd discarded and he carved it effortlessly, the dark flesh opening to reveal pieces of white swollen bulbs. Carter stared at the lily-white pockets of flesh for a moment. He had always been averse to the delicate sweet scent they delivered—not that he showed it.

'Mangosteen,' he informed her, scooping out the fruit onto her plate, but taking none for himself.

'It's delicious…' she said, popping a bulb in her mouth.

He wrinkled his nose.

'You don't like them?'

'Not particularly.'

He'd lived off them for a week—not plump and ripe, as those ones were, though, but rotten and bitter…

Carter glanced at her, pouring syrup over her breakfast, and knew he had to broach things. But first he watched as Grace took her first tentative taste of the sweet, icy, milky concoction, then went back for a second taste.

She met his eyes and actually blushed.

'What?' he asked.

'It's nothing.'

'Well, you're either having an allergic reaction or…'

'Okay, okay!' She laughed. 'Look, I'd never had sex until last night, but I'm guessing this is the perfect breakfast to have after.'

'I guess I'm about to find out.'

He hadn't really considered it in that way before.

He took a generous taste and nodded. 'Correct,' he said. 'It's definitely a good choice for…'

Then he paused, because if some foods belonged to Borneo, then this breakfast belonged to them, and he would not be partaking with another.

Not that he'd be telling her that.

Instead he moved the conversation to the reason he'd asked her out here—and it was not about sharing a romantic breakfast!

'Those guys staying at the resort—the loud ones… You were right. Their intention is to turn the place into a film set.'

She pulled a resigned face as she put down the jug. 'I thought it was just rumours,' she said. 'Or I hoped it was.'

She looked at him and he could see the disappointment clouding her eyes.

'What sort of work do you do—films or…?'

'I'm an architect.'

'Oh.' She gave a small downturned smile. 'I don't know what to say.' She looked at the lovely old banyan tree. 'Will you keep that?'

'Grace, it's my cousin Benedict who's the one in discussion with them. Arif asked me to come here to try and come up with a plan to stop him.'

'Phew!' She gave him a smile. 'So I don't have to tie myself to the tree to dissuade you?'

'You don't.'

'Is his surname Bennett too?'

Carter nodded.

'Well, his parents didn't put much thought into that.'

He found that he was smiling. 'True…' He even gave a small laugh. 'I've never thought of it before. I tend to use another B-word when referring to him. He's a bastard—always has been. His father was too.'

'Can you say no?'

'Of course,' he nodded. 'And I have repeatedly. It doesn't stop their drones going up, though, or their boats going on the water, or Benedict inviting location scouts to wade through the grounds. They want to make some wildlife adventure show—and that's just for starters. I don't want to spend the next decade in some protracted legal battle.'

'Over the house?'

'It's the land that's the real issue. The division goes right up to the resort. When I first heard, I wasn't that worried. I didn't think they'd get insurance to film here.'

'Oh, people pay a lot for danger these days.'

'It would seem so.'

She smiled then, although not at him, and he turned and saw a tree full of little silverback monkeys.

'They look like Christmas decorations.'

'Greedy ones,' he said, and made a noise to warn off one who was already reaching to jump onto the balcony.

'So,' she said, and he saw her trying to tear her eyes from

the pretty babies running along the branches, 'what are you going to do?'

'Something extreme,' Carter admitted.

For Carter, marriage was beyond extreme—and yet somehow, this morning, the impossible felt plausible.

Almost logical.

'My grandfather left the property to us both. I warned him that Benedict was a risk…'

'Yet he went ahead?'

'I guess he considered I was a risk too. He was perhaps worried I'd sell it…turn it into a resort.'

'Would you?'

'No—and I told him that. I said he should set up a trust. The locals know what needs doing. At most I expected to keep an eye from a distance…'

Once again she had him drifting from the point, he thought.

'There was a caveat in his will, though—if I marry here in Borneo, and remain married for a year, then I'll have the opportunity to buy my cousin out.'

'Do you have to live here for a year?'

'No, just marry here.'

'Was your grandfather controlling?'

'No.' He smiled at her odd response. 'He was an old romantic. I told him, clearly, that I would never marry for the sake of this place.'

'Did he put in the same clause for Benedict?'

'God, no. He'd be about to celebrate his one-year anniversary if that were the case.'

For Grace, there was something rather dreamy about sharing a delectably sweet breakfast with Carter and watching the jungle come to life. The birds were singing long before the sun spread its fingers of light. And as the violet sky merged into a vivid magenta laced with rose-gold, she saw that for once it wasn't heavy with rain. Even the few wisps of cloud were already burning off, and the morning was revealing itself to be clear and blue. The chatter from the jungle was loud, and she could almost see the trees stirring, teeming with life.

'Where's the resort from here, again?'

'That way.' He pointed.

'I can't even see the river.'

'You have to be higher up and closer to properly see it, though you can catch a glimpse of it.'

As she looked out there was a loud caw, a flock of birds rising, and then a rare silence fell — one only the jungle could provide.

Grace had noticed it—the sudden hush, as if everything had been placed on mute.

'There's a predator,' Carter said. 'The birds are giving a warning.'

'What sort of predator?

'Take your pick. A leopard, a snake...'

And if he was going to ask her to consider being his wife for a year, then he had to at least attempt to tell her why this inhospitable place mattered...even if he'd rather it did not.

'I was found close to there.'

She glanced up.

'Where you just saw those birds go up.'

'Found?'

'I was missing for a week after my family were killed. It was assumed I'd also died.'

'A *week*?'

Grace stood, the gorgeous breakfast forgotten, and went and gazed out from the balcony to look at the glimpse of river near the resort. He watched as she tried to follow the route they had taken last night, back to here. Then she looked to where he'd been found.

'It's miles from the river.'

'Days,' Carter agreed. 'The locals never gave up, though. They were sure I was out there.'

'How did they know?'

'Tracks...some ground was disturbed. They know every leaf, every bird. My father's body was recovered, and there was evidence that my mother had perished. My brother was strapped to her, so—' He faltered just briefly. 'The official search was called off, but the locals could find no physical evidence that I had been killed.'

He knew his voice was steady, yet he took a breath. The scent of mangosteen was no longer sweet, but pungent, as it had been back then, and he stood up from the table—not just to join her, but to get away from the scent.

'They kept looking. And Bashim, Arif's father, found me.'

They both looked out to where the birds had been startled, and for the first time Carter tried to fathom how an eight-year-old boy had got there.

'Bashim said I was perhaps running to get help, but that makes no sense. I was headed in the wrong direction.' He gave a wry smile. 'It would have been more sensible to wait in the boat, or even head here.'

'I doubt you were feeling very sensible.'

'I blame it on this.' He tapped the scar on his forehead. 'It would seem I fell on a rock. I used my T-shirt to bandage it.'

'Resourceful...' She smiled, but he could see tears glinting in her eyes, and he did not want sympathy, nor to unburden. He simply wanted her to understand the debt he owed to the people here.

'I was very close to death when he found me.'

'How close?'

'Judging from the wounds on my back, they thought I'd been lying there a couple of days...' He'd never told another person that. 'My back was a mess...*kalajengking*—scorpion bites—and fire ants.'

He could see her pallor...he hadn't wanted that.

'It took Bashim a couple of days to get me back to his home. He alerted the authorities and I was transferred to hospital. From the little I remember the best care I had was here. Were it not for Bashim and the people here…'

'You'd have died?'

'Certainly. Sometimes it's good not to be able to remember—'

He halted abruptly, recalling how speaking of his grandfather losing his mind had upset her the night they'd first spoken, and not wanting careless words to hurt her again.

'I apologise,' he said. 'I forgot about your mother.'

'No, no…' She put up her hand. 'They're completely separate things. You can't remember at all?'

He shook his head. 'Little bits… But really, I have no desire to. I thought when my grandfather died that I could move on for good—and then I found out my cousin is intent on destroying the place.'

'You must hate him.'

'No.' Carter shook his head. 'Certainly I don't approve of him, and I really would prefer to have nothing to do with him.'

'I'm sure he doesn't want to completely ruin it.'

Then he heard the doubt enter her voice.

'Does he…?'

'I don't think Benedict gives a damn.'

'Then your grandfather should have made better provisions—I wish to God my mother had. I never know if I'm doing the right thing by her.'

Grace's response surprised Carter. He'd thought she'd get where this was leading by now, but if anything the thought of marrying him to save the place wasn't even on her radar.

'It sounds as if you are,' he said.

'I hope so,' Grace sighed.

She was looking out to the dense jungle and she sounded as lost as he had surely felt back then.

Lost and alone.

Standing next to Grace in the silence of the early morning, for the first time he remembered hauling himself up a tree, searching for the familiar sight of the banyan. Desperate for direction…for some way out…

And he could give her that now.

'Grace?'

She turned at the sound of her name.

'You know I don't do relationships.'

'Carter…' She smiled and it reached her gorgeous green eyes. 'I think we've established that already. Look, I get it.' She gave a low laugh. 'Don't worry. I leave tomorrow…'

'What if I suggested we marry?'

Grace laughed again, only this time she rolled her eyes.

'I'm completely serious,' he insisted.

'I am not getting married to you because of some obscure clause in your grandfather's will. And if it's last night you're worried about, then don't be. I'm probably not pregnant.'

'That's a completely separate issue,' Carter interrupted. 'What if I offered you two million dollars?'

'Yes, please!' She immediately laughed once more—but then she must have seen his serious expression, because her smile and her laughter faded. 'I didn't mean that.'

'Well, I do. You need to secure your mother's future.'

'I've never once said that.'

'Am I wrong, though?'

Her silence was her answer.

'I need a solution, and fast, and if my guess is correct, you need money.'

Grace swallowed. Only now was it dawning on her that this really was a serious proposal—although not in the least the romantic kind.

'No, absolutely not. Anyway, I'm needed at home.'

'I'm aware. I have an apartment in London, and an office… I tend to spend a lot of time in New York, but in the next few months I'll be in Janana a lot, so we wouldn't be in each other's pockets.'

'That's not a marriage.'

'On paper it would be—at least enough to meet the terms of the will.'

She felt colour suffuse her cheeks at this very cold summing up.

'Grace,' he insisted. 'This is business.'

She frowned, because all the velvet of his words had gone.

He hadn't been confiding in her about his past—he'd been telling her for a reason! Now, when he spoke, he was detached, and although his grey eyes met hers, they looked *at* her rather than beyond. The change was almost indecipherable, but either their gorgeous breakfast had turned into a meeting or, she realised, he'd considered it as such all along.

'I didn't come here to discuss business or money.'

She didn't like this game…whatever he was playing.

Grace was aware she'd already been putting on a bit of a front, shielding her heart from the impact of this stunning man. And now her reckless night, her one-night stand, was offering her more, and it had utterly thrown her.

'Can we please go?' she asked.

'Of course.'

Only they were in Borneo, so it wasn't quite as simple as walking off. The little silverbacks were all waiting to pounce and have a little party with any leftovers, so she gritted her jaw as they both cleared the table away.

'I think you should ask someone a little more…' She didn't know the word she was looking for as they carried the trays down the stairs. 'I am sure there are plenty of women who would be only too happy to take your money.'

'I'm asking *you*, though, Grace.'

'Well, I wish you hadn't.'

Midway down the stairs, she simply halted, glimpsing again the precious sense of freedom she'd found last night, her own reckless abandon, the joy of discovering herself while knowing the jungle would keep her secrets.

'You've spoiled things now.'

'Or…' Carter had stopped behind her on the stairs '…I might just have made things a whole lot better.'

CHAPTER SEVEN

'YOU SEEM OFFENDED by my offer…' Carter commented as they walked across the grounds.

'Of course I am,' Grace stated, even if she did feel like some avatar that kept glitching every time the sum of money on offer popped into her head. 'I was raised to believe marriage meant something…' She paused. 'Till my dad walked out.'

'This *would* mean something,' Carter said. 'Financial security for you, less guilt for me.'

'Guilt?'

'I might not love this place; it doesn't mean I want to turn it into a movie set.' He glanced over. 'This is far less whimsical than marrying for love.'

'You think marrying for love is whimsical?'

'I do. I prefer relationships to be transactional. I don't want the responsibility for another person's safety or happiness, and I certainly don't want another person to feel responsible for mine. I told my grandfather the same. But now here we are…'

He had a point—even if she didn't agree or aspire to his cold, lonely life. She knew that responsibility well…the claw of anxiety when she thought of her mother.

She honestly hated it that she was…just a tiny bit…thinking about the advantages.

He climbed onto the boat and offered his hand. He helped her onboard then, as she took a seat, stored his laptop and the leather cylinder he always carried.

'What is that?' she asked as he carefully tucked it away with more care than his laptop. 'You take it everywhere.'

'Blueprints,' he said. 'Hand-drawn plans. And I am not going to lose them or risk them getting wet... We shan't be long.'

'It's fine. I think I'm already too late for the jungle walk...'

As he started the boat Carter didn't want to examine the relief he felt. He would never tell another person what to do, yet he'd felt a familiar dread when she'd said she was going into the jungle. The same dread he felt when Arif so casually strolled there, or Jamal said he was in the jungle with their son.

He wanted this solved so he didn't have to think of all that... so he barely had to see this land again.

And he would not lose focus on that.

Grace sat, sulking, as he started up the speedboat. 'I thought you were the one worried about your temporary lovers making demands the morning after.'

She watched his shoulders shrug in a half-laugh.

'True.'

He turned and gave her a smile that would melt the ice from the snow-caps, but she refused to return it.

'It's an offer, Grace, not a demand. You have to have been in the district for seven days before we can put in an application for marriage—that's tomorrow. Twenty-one days after that we could marry and—'

'La, la, la...' She put her fingers in her ears and then removed them. 'I am not discussing this, Carter. What happened to my no-strings one-night stand?'

'He found out she was tough.'

She wasn't, though, Grace thought. At least not when it came to Carter. Right now, her blasé reaction was all bravado.

When she'd realised he wasn't joking, his offer had stunned her. The thought of securing her mother's future had been foremost in her mind for so long, and she'd have been lying to herself to deny she'd glimpsed a solution. More worrying, though, had been a lurch of hope that their time together wasn't quite over.

She'd tried to nullify that thought, of course. To remind herself it was a financial proposal he was putting to her, rather than a romantic one. Yet with her body still tender from their night, and her heart open to a man for the first time, Grace was finding it hard to extract emotion from the business deal on offer.

Sex?

A year...?

Grace stole a look at his broad back as he casually steered, her eyes drifting over the narrow hips and firm buttocks. It was impossible not to wonder if this arrangement included bed.

A year with Carter... As if the years she'd missed out on were all condensed into a delicious one.

As if he could sense her sudden longing he glanced over his shoulder. 'Give it some consideration,' he said, before turning his attention back to the river.

Rather than doing that, she looked at the chipped coral nail varnish on her toenails, wishing she'd thought to bring nail varnish remover.

Oh, and a comb that wasn't falling apart more with each passing day.

It was easier to focus on trivialities than just sit admiring his back, and she was far too distracted by his proposal to notice they were taking a different route from last night.

'Grace?' he said, and she realised the boat had halted.

It was at that very moment she knew Carter Bennett had ruined every future lover for her.

No moment, no matter how perfect, would ever come close to this.

At the call of her name she blinked and looked up, and saw

they had come to a halt in a river that seemed to no longer exist. The brown water was spread with dark green leaves and stunning lilac flowers and the sky was the clearest blue she had seen it since her arrival.

It was as if they had landed in the jungle version of Monet's garden.

Better, even, because she wasn't gazing at an image—she was in the midst of it.

It was truly a halcyon moment, the silence broken only by the gentle lap of the water against the boat.

'Where are we?' she asked him.

'Close to the resort,' he said. 'The tour boats are too big to get down here.' He reached into the water and plucked one of the flowers and handed it to her. 'Water hyacinths.'

'Stunning.'

'They're taking over,' he said.

In truth they were invasive, and clogging the rivers, but he chose not to spoil it for her because, yes, they were indeed beautiful.

Only that wasn't why he had brought her here.

Carter stood up, scanning the trees, then his eyes locked on one close to the riverbank. 'Grace...' he started.

'Please...'

Grace tried to halt him. She couldn't, though, because sitting in a river of lilac flowers, her body tender and her memory fresh from being bedded by him, she was having enough trouble designating this a holiday romance...enough trouble holding on to her heart. So instead, she stared back down to the flower, to the gorgeous petals, their orange tips like peacock feathers.

'I don't want to discuss this any further.'

'Shh...'

'Excuse me?' she checked, affronted at being shushed.

But then she saw that he wasn't looking at her. Instead he was staring out, holding up one hand as Felicity did when she wanted them to be quiet.

'There.' He pointed and she followed the line of his finger. What they'd been discussing faded. 'See the nest?'

She couldn't.

'Come here,' he said quietly, summoning her, his eyes set on the trees as, a little unsteadily, she stood too, and walked over. 'There's movement. Right there.'

Oh! She'd been looking into the distance, but he was pointing to a tree close to the river's edge, and there was a huge nest halfway up.

'See?' he checked, and Grace nodded excitedly as a little head popped up. 'They're waking up.'

The tiny head bobbed down again, but not a moment later two arms stretched up, large hands holding a tiny baby orangutan in the air. She couldn't see the mother, just her arms and hands around her infant, the little baby gazing down. It was such a tranquil moment, a precious moment… A mother raising her infant in the air, playing with her baby as any mother would. Then the baby disappeared from sight, still held in loving arms.

'That was incredible…'

It was a relief for Grace to have a reason to let out a little of the emotion that she'd kept pent up since this morning—to cry a little and wipe the tears with the back of her hands.

'I'd almost given up seeing one in the wild. We've been looking for them all week.'

'They're hard to find—the females make a new nest most nights.'

'What about the males?'

'Oh, they're lazy—more often than not they use the discarded nests.'

Grace gave a soft laugh. 'Typical!'

'Or practical,' Carter countered, and then she felt him looking at her. 'Grace, I may be male, but unlike our primate friends I am *not* lazy. I have built my own nest and feathered it very nicely. I don't mind feathering yours if you'll join me for a year.'

'I think I ought to get back.'

'Are you sure…?'

She was about to nod, but then realised he wasn't suggesting they stay to discuss his proposal, just asking if she wanted to watch the nest for a little longer.

'They'll come down at some point, though it might take a while.'

He was completely content to wait, and she could not understand how he could make such a calculating offer, then moments later stand in silent awe, patiently watching these beautiful creatures.

It was Grace who brought up the topic again. 'I don't see how it could work.' Her cheeks were on fire. She was embarrassed to admit she was thinking about it. 'A fake marriage.'

'It happens all the time.' Carter assured her. 'We'd get an application for marriage here, then fly to Kuala Lumpur… We can meet my lawyer there, work out the details, draw up an NDA and such, then agree on a prenup.'

'In English, please?'

'We try to come to a deal we can both agree on and ensure nobody else finds out.'

He halted as the little head of the baby orangutan peeked out again, as if checking that all was clear.

Gosh, it was so human-looking, so tiny.

'Carter…' she gulped '…what if I *am* pregnant.'

His response was abrupt, even stern. 'This proposal has *nothing* to do with that.'

'But what if I am, though?'

'Shall we cross that bridge if we come to it?'

She looked at the little head, peering from the nest, and

knew that no matter what Carter and his lawyer might prefer, she'd already made her decision.

'I *shall* be crossing that bridge, Carter,' she warned him. 'Should the issue arise.'

'Your choice.' He nodded. 'So long as you know we'd still have no future.' His eyes flashed a warning. 'I'll build you a nice bridge, though. Well maintained.'

He took out all the emotion—and, ridiculously, it helped.

She was trying so hard to think of this in practical terms. Using every ounce of logic to stop her heart from dreaming of dangerous scenarios where there was at least some possibility that there was more behind this offer. Some glimmer that this contract marriage held a whisper of hope for them both.

But he'd made it abundantly clear that it didn't.

They waited another ten, maybe fifteen minutes, with the occasional glimpse of hands or a little head, and then there was something she had to ask.

'Would we...?' Her voice was croaky, so she cleared it. 'Does this sham marriage involve us sleeping together?'

It was almost a ridiculous question. Her body was alive to him, she was almost fighting not to move closer to him, and yet it was so vital she asked it. She had collapsed beneath him. One night in his bed had taken her to places she had never known existed.

What would a year together entail?

And what happened when boredom set in and the naïve woman no longer amused him?

Before she even entertained the idea these were details she had to know.

The answers terrified her so.

'Benedict is going to throw everything at me—as I intended with him,' he said. 'So in KL at least we would need to share a suite. It would look odd otherwise.'

'And a bed?'

'Of course—although with that said, sex should never be a chore,' Carter said. 'I certainly don't want duty sex.'

'So you'd go without for a year?' she challenged.

'God, no.' He met her gaze, then. 'If you don't want sex to be a part of our agreement that's fine. I'll agree to be discreet.'

She felt a tremble in her lips and pinched them, reminded herself again that this was a contract...not real.

Then she looked at his strong profile and imagined all that maleness cooped up in a marriage he didn't really want. And she knew that unless she set down some strong rules there was the chance for true heartbreak ahead.

'If you sleep with another woman, then know you'll never again sleep with me.'

'Fine.' He was still staring intently at the nest. 'I'll have Jonathon add that to the contract.'

God, he was brutal. Nothing moved or fazed him.

'Along with my agreement to be discreet.'

He turned his abruptly to her and she saw the male he was, the snap of possession in his eyes, and Grace swore to herself that she would never mistake that look for love.

It gave her the strength to speak on. 'If the relationship falls apart in the bedroom...'

'I've *never* fallen apart in the bedroom.'

'I'm just saying,' Grace retorted calmly, 'that if we go our separate ways, then I too shall be discreet.'

A slight incredulous smile spread over his lips. 'You were a virgin until recently.'

'Thank you for showing me all I was missing out on,' she said, and gave him a tight smile.

She was being brave in words, but she doubted she could ever be so brave in deed. Still, she would not let him see that.

'So we'd have that added to the contract too.'

'Fine.'

'*If* I go ahead.'

They stood quietly. The occasional light motion of the boat

meant the tops of their arms brushed every now and again, just a little, and her skin flared at each brief contact, refused to settle.

God, she was really deeply considering it...

'What would I tell Violet?' She could hear herself almost panting, as if on some frantic hunt, stopping breathlessly for clues along the way.

'That we met, fell in love... You can't tell her the truth.'

'I know.' Grace nodded. 'But she knows me. Knows I wouldn't rush into something like this.' She blinked a couple of times. 'I don't think she'd believe me.'

'Then make it so,' Carter said.

She felt his head turn and then his mouth close to her ear.

'Tell her I asked you to marry me in a river of lilac flowers...'

Her breathing was so shallow now she was almost dizzy.

'That we made love in a boat and you said yes...'

She was shaking—perhaps from standing in the morning sun?

Or was it the thought of the two million dollars that would change both her and her mother's life?

Or just lust and desire?

'Does Arif know about the will?' Grace asked. 'Is that why you were arguing?'

'No.' Carter shook his head. 'And we weren't arguing.'

'You looked like thunder when you came out of his office.'

He rolled his eyes. 'If Arif were a woman, we'd have been over years ago. He's that person you can't say no to...or you can't stop worrying about.'

Grace just laughed.

'I think you mean Arif is family.'

'Oh, no. Believe me, I have nothing to do with any of them, aside from legally.'

'I mean family of the heart.' Grace smiled. 'Like Violet is to me...'

She didn't finish, seeing his attention completely on the nest and intently alert.

'She's moving,' Carter said.

And Grace blinked, remembered why they were there, and remembered that this moment—watching a mother orang-utan leave her nest—was what she'd been aching for all week.

It still was.

Yet somehow it was made better because she was sharing it with him.

'Where's the baby?' she asked.

'Shh!' he said.

This time Grace didn't take offence.

'It will be with her,' he told her. Then he put an arm around her, pulled her closer as he pointed with his free hand. 'See beneath her arm? Do you want the binoculars?'

'No.'

She really was dreadful with them. But, more, she liked seeing things with her own eyes, and, yes, liked being so close to him, hearing his voice, low and quiet, so as not to carry on the still air.

'I see it.'

Sure enough, she could just make out the infant, cling-ing on as the mother stretched an impossibly long arm and reached up.

'She's coming this way,' Carter told her, and they both stood in utter silence, watching the mother move from branch to branch with ease, getting closer to the riverbank with each agile swing.

Grace had to press her lips together. It was simply incred-ible to watch. And there was no need for binoculars, because she came further down, close to the river's edge, till she hung by one hand, no more than a few arms' lengths away from where they stood together in the boat.

'She's watching us,' Carter said.

'I know! I'm trying not to make eye contact,' Grace whispered.

'They don't mind much,' he said. 'They communicate that way.' Then he added, 'And she's not worried by us.'

No, the mother wasn't worried, for she hung there, calmly eating fruit, as the little baby moved onto her chest, boldly peering out at them with huge black eyes, the sun catching on its soft tufts of auburn and gold hair.

'Is it a boy or a girl?' Grace whispered.

'Can't tell,' he said. 'It's very young.'

'How young?'

'A couple of months.'

Then the mother lowered her head, and in the tenderest, simplest gesture she kissed the top of her baby's downy head, then lifted the little one up high on her shoulder, as if she were about to wind her.

And then it was over.

Almost.

The mother calmly dropped down from the tree and walked into the forest, the little baby peering over its mother's shoulder back at them.

'It's so content…' Grace said, stunned at what they'd witnessed.

But then she felt Carter's arm tighten its hold a fraction and she looked up at him, wondering if he was alerting her to something. But, no, it was more as if something had alerted *him*, for even though he stood right beside her, he looked a million miles away.

Carter, in fact, was twenty-seven years in the past, staring at the baby orangutan's huge round eyes that looked back at him just as Hugo's had that last day.

But there was a forgotten moment that had returned…

Hugo holding his fat starfish hand out to him.

Carter had known exactly what his brother's gesture meant.

'Wait!' he'd called, opening his father's ice box, taking

the cold silver teething ring and jumping onto the riverbank.
'There you go, Ulat,' he'd said, handing Hugo his beloved
teething ring, gently talking to his little brother as he'd grasped
it, ruffling his soft hair, seeing his contented smile...

Then, as if black tar was being thrown over him, the idyl-
lic moment was tainted.

He should have taken Hugo from his mother...carried him
back to the boat.

God, this was no memory to stand and savour. Instead he
stood there hollowed out with regret.

The only solace he could find as he recalled it was that he'd
never know the pain of such loss again.

Ever.

'That was incredible...'

Grace's voice pulled him back to the present and, realising
his arm was still around her, Carter removed it, telling himself
he'd merely been trying to point out the wildlife.

'I can't believe how close we were.'

'It's very quiet here,' Carter said, and cleared his throat,
trying to sound normal while still taken aback by that emer-
gence of the final memory of his mother and brother. 'There's
little to disturb them.'

'What will happen if your cousin does get his way?'

'That's my concern. I didn't bring you here to influence
your decision.'

Carter would not let emotions override her thinking—they
were a currency he did his level best not to deal in.

'Your decision should be based on financial security and
providing for your mother. The debt to the people here is my
own.'

'Debt?'

'There's a saying here: *Hutang emas boleh dibayar, hutang budi dibawa mati.* One can pay back the loan of gold,

but one dies in debt for ever to those who are kind. Unfortunately for me, it's true.'

'I'm sure they don't see it as a debt.'

'Perhaps not a debt, but I do feel obliged.' He saw Grace frown, and then qualified. 'I want to do the right thing, and then finally I can move on.'

'I do too,' Grace admitted, her own words surprising her. 'I don't see it as a debt, though, or even an obligation.'

She wanted to do the best by her mother and she wanted to live her life. This gave her a chance to do both.

'I don't know if can do this, though.'

'That's why there are lawyers…that's why we're not running away to Vegas. If we get the application in then we have three weeks to work things out.'

She nodded.

'Grace, do you love me?'

Her response was immediate. 'Of course not.'

Only Grace recognised her own tone. It was the same one she used when asked if she cared about or missed her father.

She didn't love Carter, of course—she didn't know him—but she stared at the rainforest in the bright morning and knew that she had to stay silent. For she could think of nothing better than knowing this contrary man more.

He clearly hadn't finished checking she could match his cold heart, though. He had another question for her.

'And you understand that I'll never love you?'

How did one even begin to answer that?

'You've made that very clear.'

She took a breath, looked at the beautiful lilacs. There was more tranquillity here than she had ever known, and finally enough peace to think deeply.

Serenity?

Not quite.

But it was enough that she'd found the touchstone of her heart.

'I want real love.' She looked out to the jungle that pulsed with life, to the flowers, to the sky, and she told him the truth. 'I'm so tired of loving people who are incapable of loving me.'

He frowned.

'I'm talking about my father.' She could feel her lips stretch, her chin tremble, but she forced herself to push on. 'My mother.'

'She's unwell.'

'I know—and, believe me, I've had to tell myself that a lot of times over the years.' She took a breath. 'I want someone who can love me fully.'

'It's a no, then?'

'Can I finish?'

She thought of security for her mother and being able to provide the best life she could give her. Of how, if her mother was cared for, she'd get the chance to live her own best life.

Find herself.

Her passions.

She looked over to Carter and, as cold and matter-of-fact his proposal was, it excited her too. Last night she had found all she had missed out on. He'd brought something out in her she hadn't even known existed.

'I shan't be falling in love with a man incapable of loving me back. So, yes.' She nodded. 'I do want to do this.'

'Two million dollars… A wardrobe…'

'I'd need to get to London regularly.'

'Once we're married, I can base myself there.'

It was a minor detail to him, Grace realised. He could up-root to wherever he liked on a whim.

'We'll work out the details of the contract, but…' He seemed to think for a moment, as if pondering what else might be required. 'I think we're both getting a good deal. I like you.' He said it as if it surprised him. 'Although, of course, by the end of the year we'll be desperate to never see each other again.'

Grace hoped so!

She really, really hoped so...

CHAPTER EIGHT

'WHERE WE MET…' Carter said, as they walked through Kuala Lumpur airport and passed the bench where he'd found her sleeping. 'For when you tell Violet.'

'Check,' Grace said, as if she was only now remembering, when that moment was already etched on her heart.

There was a car and driver waiting for them. After a week in the jungle the lights and sights of a busy city late evening were overwhelming. The car was moving at speed through the streets, and there were just so many people.

Carter, clearly delighted to be back in civilisation, had his diary up on a screen and was talking to his assistant, confirming appointments, meetings, flights…

'What ring size are you?' he asked.

'I've no idea. Why?'

He rolled his eyes and got back to his call.

For Grace there was a feeling of excitement that she hadn't expected, and she told him the same as they approached the luxurious hotel. 'I thought I'd feel guilty,' she admitted.

'Why?' Carter frowned.

'It seems wrong. Well, it *seemed* wrong.' She thought back to her abhorrence when he'd first suggested it, yet even before he'd dropped her back at the resort she'd turned things around.

Her last night spent with the group had been incredible.

Arif had been the guide, with Felicity steering the boat,

and the pygmy elephants had been at the riverbank as if to wave goodbye...

And then Carter had collected her in the morning.

The story was that she would be working for Carter, collating data for his legal team.

'Thanks for coming on board,' Arif had said as he'd farewelled her. 'I've given some of the data to Carter, but here are my contact details.'

Felicity had even hugged her!

'I'm going to miss the jungle,' she admitted.

'I shan't,' he said, climbing out of the car.

He offered his hand as she went to get out, just as he had on the speedboat, and gave her a begrudging smile.

'Okay, some parts were good.'

Even checking in to such a sumptuous place didn't daunt, when usually it would have, even though for her it was quite an event.

As Carter sat at a desk and spoke with the guest services manager about their upcoming stay Grace sat, sipping pink tea and nibbling gorgeous wafers. And instead of feeling intimidated by the glamorous staff and gorgeous guests, she sat in her black shorts and dusky pink top and called the nursing home.

There was an agency nurse on, whom Grace didn't know, but she told her that her mother was at singing practice.

'Is she settling in?'

'She seems very happy. Maggie's in tomorrow—she'll be able to tell you more.'

'Thanks.'

It was such a relief to know she was okay, and Grace sat back, looking out at the dark city and to the glittering skyline.

'Grace?'

She looked up to find Carter standing there. 'They're still getting the suite ready.'

'Oh.' She'd have expected them to have it ready and

waiting for him from the way they were fawning over him.
'No problem.'

'We'll go up to the bar.'

'Carter, no!'

She pointed to her attire, thought of her hair, but he was already walking towards the elevators. Even the doors parted to his instant command, and she stepped into the dimly lit space.

'I'm hardly dressed for a bar.'

'I'm not waiting in Reception.'

'It's dark in here,' she commented, looking around.

'Subtle.' He smiled. 'The corridors are the same—hell when you've had a drink.'

He made the whole thing a little easier, somehow, although as they stepped into a gorgeous dimly lit corridor she tried not to think of Carter and the glamorous beauties who had surely walked this luxurious path with him before.

'Mr Bennett.' He was welcomed with a smile by the greeter. 'Madam.'

They were led outside to some high tables set with pretty lights, where beautiful people were sipping cocktails, enjoying the balmy night. His entrance did not go unnoticed. For the first time in her life Grace felt heads turn as she walked by, and certainly they were for Carter. But then, as they walked to their table, Grace literally stopped.

'Oh, my gosh!'

She'd heard of the Petronas Towers, had seen them in pictures and had been planning to visit them, but standing on the rooftop bar, seeing them close up, as if two giant crystal decanters had been placed in the sky, was simply incredible.

'Like a new moon,' Carter said, standing beside her, his hand around her waist. 'It's better if you don't see it the first time through glass.'

'Is that why you brought me here?'

She couldn't take her eyes off them, yet she had to as

they were being led to a private area, a velvet rope being moved aside.

'Thank you,' she said as he gestured for her to take the stool that faced the towers. 'For giving me the best view.'

Carter could have chosen to debate that point.

Her hair was heavy with ringlets, her T-shirt was falling off her shoulder, and her face was glowing. His view was excellent! Her smile and her eyes were bright. He was so used to just a bland reaction when he brought a date here, and yet Grace was enthralled.

Her enthusiasm had him revealing more. 'They were my inspiration.'

'To be an architect?'

He nodded. 'I used to look out for them when I came home on vacation.'

'To see your grandfather?'

'Of course.'

But as he turned his head to follow her gaze, Carter was starting to recall times long before that.

'My family used to come most summers, but we rarely stopped here. My parents hated the city, but I begged them to take me up. I knew I wanted to design something like that even then.'

'Cognac, sir?'

Carter nodded, and the fact that the waiter knew this nettled Grace a little. As 'madam' was handed a menu, she stared at it, unseeing. There were just too many reminders that, as special as this night might feel, it was commonplace for him.

Carter tried to help with her selection. 'The gin *pahit* is excellent here.'

'Better not.' She glanced at him. 'Mother's ruin and all that. I'm sure I'll be fine, but...' She gave the menu better attention, pleased to see there was something familiar. 'Mangosteen Mocktail, please.'

Grace smiled, only he didn't return it.

God, please don't let me be pregnant, Grace thought.

She rather guessed he was thinking the same thing.

'I am going to Janana soon,' he said.

'Where?'

'The Middle East,' he explained. 'I have a big project there.'

'Oh?'

'Jonathon, my lawyer, is flying in, but before he gets here there'll be time to sort out a few things...'

He paused the conversation as their drinks arrived and the waiter placed a gorgeous pink drink on the table before her.

It was soft, yet fruity, and so icy and delicious. 'It's like peaches.' She pushed the glass towards him, and then frowned, because he seemed about to decline. 'Look, I'm sorry I brought it up.' She was awkward. 'I just don't think I should be drinking.'

'It's fine.'

As if to prove he wasn't annoyed that she might be pregnant he reached for the glass and, almost reluctantly, took a taste.

He screwed up his nose. 'Not for me.'

'I thought you liked mangosteen?'

'No.'

'But we had them...' Her voice trailed off as she remembered he had only peeled one for her, rather than have any himself, and when she'd asked had said he didn't particularly like them.

Carter took a sip of cognac, as if to rinse his mouth,

It was a sickly taste, a familiar taste—only it wasn't this sweet, fruity version he was recalling, but the rotten, decomposing fruit on the jungle floor that had been most of his sustenance for a week.

He took another sip of cognac, looked up at her eyes. He

wanted to tell her that memories were starting to come back, his recollections becoming more frequent by the day. Tell her how he'd hoped things would change now they were out of the jungle.

That wasn't part of the deal they'd made, though.

Yet the taste of that damn drink was still on his tongue and churning in his stomach.

As she reached to take the glass he told her what was wrong. 'They were the only food I could find when I was missing.'

She looked at the glass, the condensation trickling down the side, and then up to him. 'You should have said that morning. I wouldn't have asked you to peel one.'

'We were meant to be a one-off then.'

'Yes.'

'And I'd only just remembered then.'

'I'll order something else.'

'No, no,' he said. 'Finish your drink. I just thought it better to say…'

'Before it becomes my nightly treat?'

She made him smile, even with the sickly scent still in the air, and he watched as she called for the waiter and asked him to take the glass away.

'Is everything okay?' the waiter checked.

It was Carter who answered. 'It's fine.' He'd just got a message. 'I believe our suite is ready.'

Their suite was so much more than a suite—it was beyond stunning. They stepped into a candlelit wonder, where the darkened lounge room showed the incredible skyline. But Grace loved it that he'd taken her to the roof to witness the towers first.

'Wow!' she kept saying as she explored the beautiful suite, trying out the low chairs, even dipping her toes in the sunken pool by the floor-to-ceiling windows.

* * *

Carter headed to the dressing room just off the master suite.

'Passport,' he called, as he put his own in the safe, checking too that the rings he'd ordered were in there, but without sentiment.

He tried to avoid the churn of feelings as he placed the black pouch in there. Wished to God that the damn teething ring had stayed beneath ground.

'Grace,' he said again. 'Passport.'

'It'll be fine.'

'Said the woman who fell asleep and dropped hers…'

'True.'

He was surprised that after several modes of transport and many hours with her he wasn't aching to be alone, or annoyed by her running commentary as she flitted from room to room, but he caught her tension as she stepped into the candlelit master bedroom.

She gave a nervous laugh. 'We'll spend half the night blowing out all the candles.'

'I don't think you have to worry about that.'

'Here,' Grace said, handing over her passport and then heading back out.

She didn't linger in the bedroom. The vast white bed was daunting. It was so beautifully prepared… There were 'his and her' kimonos draped either side, and just a sensual look to it that made her throat feel tight.

A mocking voice told her that Carter would soon grow tired of his very inexperienced lover, especially in surroundings as sophisticated as this.

It was all so subtly sexy and dark. Like Carter, she thought as she went behind a glass wall and saw more candles placed around a deep stone bath already filled with soapy water.

'Look,' she said as Carter wandered through, and dipped her hand in. 'It's hot!' she exclaimed. 'How?'

'They would have prepared it while we were at the bar,' Carter said, breaking the romantic mood and flicking the lights on.

'I wish you hadn't done that,' Grace muttered, seeing not just her tatty toiletry bag on the gleaming marble, but her tatty reflection in the equally gleaming mirror. And, yes, she looked as if she'd been dragged through the jungle backwards. 'My hair!' she groaned, for it seemed to move as one. 'Are the mirrors in Sabah kinder?'

Carter found the mirrors kinder here.

The world was in neat order—unlike in the jungle.

He liked Grace brightly lit, so he could see the dusting of freckles on her nose, and how her T-shirt gaped as she leant forward and moaned about her eyebrows. He liked her bare feet on the marble floors…

'I'm going shopping tomorrow,' she told him, taking tweezers from her toiletry bag.

'I'll leave a credit card for you. Or charge it…'

'I didn't mean that.' She stopped plucking her eyebrows and caught his eye in the mirror. 'I was always going to get rid of these clothes and buy some new things.'

'I don't think the high street is going to cut it.'

Her eyes narrowed. 'Are you saying I'm to be more "Carter Bennett's fiancée" suitable?'

'I'm saying exactly that.' He nodded. 'Tomorrow night I have to meet with a senior financier.'

'Am I to make small talk with his wife?'

'No, I shall be doing most of the talking. Simi's the one who I need to sweet talk—you get the husband.' He watched her get back to her eyebrows and could not resist adding, 'They're in the top one hundred of the most successful, beautiful people.'

'Shut up!' She smiled. 'Are you serious?'

'Very.' he nodded.

'If you're already so rich, why do you need to impress a financier?'

'Because I intend to stay rich,' he retorted. 'Get some nice clothes, and whatever else you need…'

She might have been wholly offended, but staring at her woolly hair and dusty clothes she felt a shiver of excitement. It felt as if she'd spent for ever dressed in yoga pants, with her hair in a ponytail, having dinner in front of the television. Rarely going out, let alone dating.

This wasn't dating, though, Grace reminded herself.

Carter began to strip his top off—as uninhibited as that— and she wondered if she was about to be summoned to the bath…

Could you use condoms in water?

She had no clue. So for something to do she opened up all the freebies and brushed her teeth with a very nice brush, selected all the lovely shampoos. She was delaying, nervous…

'Grace…'

He turned her around. He was naked from the hips up, and he wiped a little toothpaste from her lip.

And she thought he must seriously hate mangosteen, because his gaze had changed, and it would seem her mouth was kissable now.

This wasn't love, she thought as their mouths met, but nor was it shame. It was finding out how good a kiss could be, discovering her body, feeling wanted and sexy when she'd wondered if that side of her even existed.

His tongue tasted of cognac, and when it mingled with hers she tasted mint. And her hands were on his chest, feeling the dark hair, the flat nipples. And she didn't want this kiss to end. But he was more measured than she…pulling that sexy mouth back from her own.

'Why don't we lose the jungle?' Carter suggested, pulling at the hem of her dusky and also rather dusty pink top.

The tops of her thighs ached and her breasts felt tight with anticipation as he lifted her arms and removed her top, tossing it towards a basket. She watched her very tatty bra fly that way too, and then he left it for Grace to take care of the rest. Possibly because he needed to be naked as much as she.

Although not for the reasons she'd first thought.

'Enjoy,' he said, taking her hand and helping her into the bath.

She watched a little bemused as he headed to the shower, and perhaps he saw her blink of surprise.

'Did I tell you I'm not romantic?'

'Many times.'

'That means I don't do candlelit baths. I'm going in here.'

'Bastard!' She laughed and lay back, still semi turned on, but finally relaxed, letting the fragrant water wrap around her body. Sometimes her eyes would open and drift to look at his magnificent physique, his lean legs, the indentations at the side of his taut buttocks. And it was intimate to watch him from a distance, to see the thick length that had been inside her and to feel her throat go tight. He turned and she saw the scars on his back... She closed her eyes on the vision of scorpions and fire ants, knowing he'd hate the tears that had suddenly filled her eyes.

He turned off the water, came out and wrapped a towel around his hips, and flicked through all the toiletries. He started to lather up several days' worth of growth on his chin, not even bothering to look at her when she asked, 'Is there any more conditioner? My hair's all knotted.'

'Book a hairdresser tomorrow.'

'Please!' Grace mumbled, lying back in the bath and letting the water wash over her, knowing he couldn't possibly understand how awful it was going to be to face a hairdresser somewhere as gorgeous as here. She usually trimmed her own hair, and the humid air really had wreaked havoc with it, as well as the near toothless comb.

* * *

Carter was now watching Grace.

The efficient extractor fans meant he didn't even need to wipe the mirror to shave. Still, rather than his own reflection there was a far more appealing sight in the mirror, as Grace lay back in the bath and floated. Her hair fanned out, her eyes closed, and he saw her usually pale skin was pink from the warm water. The dispersing bubbles revealed her soft breasts and his eyes moved to the dark triangle of hair.

He thought of their one night...the heat they had made.

He understood a little of what Grace meant when she'd said she kept expecting shame to kick in... In Carter's case, though, he was waiting for regret to arrive.

Waiting to rue the offer he'd made.

Even as they shared the bathroom he kept waiting to feel as if she was invading his space, and yet it was Carter who wanted to invade hers... To climb into the bath and feel that slippery body...to be with her again. *Now!*

'What about this?' he asked and she glanced over. 'It says "Hair Masque".'

She sat up and held out an impatient hand, but just as she grabbed it he pulled it away. 'Please...' he reminded her.

'Please,' she said, and with slippery hands tried to open it.

She soon gave in and now it was she who held it out, for him to open.

'Please!' she repeated, and then she caught his eye and they both smiled.

This was the smile she gave only now and then, and he found himself giving back a new smile.

Then the smiles faded, but their eyes remained locked.

The water was still, as was Grace, and there was no fan powerful enough to erase the unseen mist of desire descending.

As he handed Grace the opened hair masque he saw that her

flush was darker and that the nipples that had been flat were now puckering and pointing as if the steaming water was cold.

'Do you need help?' he offered.

Carter loved the way her neck corded in tension as she nodded.

He didn't do this, Carter reminded himself as he collected a comb from the selection on offer. Usually women arrived dressed and scented...or he woke to the spritzed version.

'Move.'

He gestured and she scooted forward, and as he climbed into the bath behind her there was just a little slosh as his six-foot-three frame lowered. She leant over to survey the spillage, her skin gleaming, wet, and he reached for her waist, pulled her between his legs.

No, he had never done this, Carter thought, massaging the thick cream through her hair, then slowly combing it through.

'My comb broke,' Grace explained, feeling a little embarrassed, but far less so than she would have been under the critical eye of a hairdresser tomorrow. 'Well, it kept snapping,' she told him. 'I'm nervous about tomorrow,' she admitted, somehow finding it easier to talk as he combed her hair, to admit her thoughts. 'Not just about the hairdresser.'

'Why?'

'I don't know anything about make-up, clothes...not lately anyway. I feel like there's a big gap in my knowledge—a six-year yoga-pants-and-baggy-T-shirt-shaped gap.'

'Let the stylists here help?' he suggested.

She nodded, but the gentle mood changed when he must have hit a rather difficult knot. 'Ow!'

'Sorry...'

He paused long enough to kiss her shoulder and the last traces of awkwardness and embarrassment simply faded away. Even if he thrilled her, there was something incredibly relaxing about Carter—a quiet knowledge that he wouldn't be doing this unless he chose to. He wouldn't be combing her hair and holding her between his thighs for any reason other than that he wanted to.

And she wanted him there too.

'I'm not used to long hair,' he explained as he resumed.

And perhaps it relaxed him, too, because he seemed to be dwelling on that thought.

He'd only ever combed his own hair.

Certainly he wasn't used to combing long, thick, curly hair until it hung heavy, smooth and glossy down her back.

'There,' he said.

But as she went to turn around, he pulled her to lie back against him. Lifted her hair so it lay over his shoulder rather than in the water.

'The packet says fifteen minutes.'

And he used every one.

Several of them spent with large slippery hands sliding over her breasts, toying with the peaks.

Grace lay there, feeling him so turned on behind her. She ached to turn around, to touch him, too, and yet it was bliss to just lie there.

To feel one hand slide down and part her legs a little, to rest her thighs against his and for his fingers to explore her.

She turned her head and he kissed her mouth. 'I want...' She was tense with the need to turn, but too laden with pleasure to move.

She felt guilty, because the focus was so much on her own pleasure, was unable to accept that the pleasure was also his.

'God, you fight,' Carter said, and he gripped her thighs closed with his, and then there were no more kisses, just moans as she leant her head forward and beneath the water gave in to the pleasure that rippled through her.

His thighs parted and she folded, clutching her knees, sated.

As he climbed out, he offered his hand. 'Give me a mo-ment…' Her legs were shaky, but Carter wasn't waiting.

'Come on,' he instructed. 'We need to rinse your hair.'

She would have gone to his bed with the masque still in, every thought except for him seemed to have floated out of her head.

He took the gold shower attachment from the bath and she knelt on the towel he had dropped to the floor a little later than the fifteen minutes stated on the pack.

No regret as to her decision to come here.

Still no shame.

None.

'We could go back in the shower,' Grace suggested as she leant over the bath.

'We could,' he said, his voice with a thick edge, 'but then you'd have to move and I don't want you to.'

She felt his finger run down the length of her spine, opened her eyes to her hair dripping into the bath, to the feeling of his deft fingers in her scalp, then the tug as he squeezed the water out.

'Do you want to go to bed?' he offered. 'Or…?'

'Here,' she said, her voice a bit of a squeak. She was just not wanting to lose the exquisite feel of his hands low on her back, sliding to her hips and moving her just a fraction. 'Just here,' she affirmed.

'Good,' he said.

She rested her head on her forearm, almost shaking with trepidation as he leant over her body and turned off the water. The feel of him aroused and erect matched her own swol-len pleasure. She could feel his hand moving down, closing around himself, and she felt a desperate, delicious impatience flood her veins.

'Hold on,' he said.

And that desperate, delicious feeling flicked into frustra-tion as he remembered to keep both of them safe this time.

He stretched to the counter behind them, his other hand on her stomach, and there should have been relief that he'd remembered protection, or a little quip about the thoughtful placement of condoms, but the only thing she could think of was the gap placed between their bodies, the air that did not belong there.

Then he was back, his knees between her calves, his hands on her breasts. 'Look,' he said, and she lifted her head. But he corrected her. 'To the side.'

She could see them in the mirror.

Grace barely recognised herself. Her skin was pink, her eyes dark and wide as they watched his hands on her breasts as they move to her waist.

'Oh...' She was shivering—a little from the cool air on her wet skin and a lot from the sight of Carter kneeling up, holding himself, rolling a condom on.

She raised herself higher, her bottom pressing backwards.

'Are you still sore?'

'No,' she said, as he slid in his fingers.

She had been prepared to perfection, and his deft check was soon completed, fingers replaced. She felt the nudge of him.

'Maybe a bit,' she gasped, realising she was still a little raw from their first time. But the return to bliss was swift. 'Don't stop!'

'Shh,' he said, as if he were concentrating, and then she realised the effort he was taking to enter her slowly, felt the tension in his body and heard it in his breathing as he eased in.

Certainly it hurt less than the first time, and it allowed her to fully feel the stretch. And then he repeated the thrust, and repeated it, until it was she who moved her hips back a little, wanting more, ever more. Because he'd moved deeper, and she felt him nudge at her cervix, and she groaned at the decadent places he took her, slowly and very deliberately,

Each thrust had her closing her eyes tighter, and then he

took her hips and moved her, and Grace found that she was back to looking in the mirror.

'You like watching?'

She nodded, as he confirmed another thing she hadn't known about herself, and then he pulled out, enough to move them so that she was kneeling facing the mirrored wall, with him behind her. He entered her again, and there was nothing to lean on, but he guided her arms behind her, so they were locked under his, and she watched as his hands explored her body, both saw and felt the pleasure he gave. And then his cheek came to hers, and he watched them for a moment, his hand in her most intimate place.

'My knees hurt,' she told him, because there was pleasure in every other pore.

And he laughed. And, carefully holding the sheath, removed himself again, spinning her to face him.

'I'm going on the pill,' she blurted out in her frustration.

How she wanted his skin…even the tiniest of barriers felt too much.

For Carter, her words took him back to the feel of her naked and tight around him, to the one time he'd been careless, and he adored how his inexperienced lover already craved that again.

He had never, ever wanted this closeness, this much of another person—not just the press of her naked on his chest, her hands on his shoulders, but on his back, where the scars were no longer a novelty, or something to avoid, just a part of him.

He kissed her hard, relieved that she did not know that he did not always kiss as passionately as this, that she was unaware that the feel of her wet hair on his face and sex on the bathroom floor, as inconvenient and hard as the marble felt, was a new discovery for him too.

He was a controlled lover, although he was losing control

now—but then she could not know how rare this was, because she was falling apart too.

Her arms were locked around his neck, and she could feel his hot breath. His movements were urgent and intense, and then there was an incredible sense of being still. She was trying not to tremble, she felt the energy that was coming, and yet her body was already alight.

Grace gasped and screwed her eyes closed as he held her steady, moaned as her orgasm met his. He shuddered in a breathless shout and then moved her slowly, tender and aching, the length of him.

She could hear their breathing, her own heart and possibly even his. It was the most incredible, selfish feeling. Such a rich, giddy pleasure, and yet it felt like a shared one.

'You're cold...' he observed, and it took a moment for Grace to acknowledge that she was.

For the first time since she'd landed in Malaysia her skin was cool, and with her hair still drenched she really was shivering.

'Finally!'

Her legs were almost numb as she stood, and he took her hand and led her through the stunning rooms.

The bed was already turned back and it was such a relief to sink into it.

'What are you doing?' she asked as he went to the dressing room.

'I meant to...'

He came out with a box—a flat black velvet and rather large box—and sat on the bed and unclipped it.

There were so many things about Grace that surprised him, thought Carter, and her reaction to the black velvet tray did too. For even though there were diamonds, sapphires, emeralds and rubies, and even though most of the women he'd dated would have squealed, she just stared.

She was like no one he'd met.

And the clinical proposal was a little nicer than he'd intended, what with the candles putting themselves to bed around them, fizzing out one by one, and her chest still flushed from orgasm and her soft, naked breasts a diversion for him as she stared at the selection.

'Choose one.'

'We haven't even spoken to the lawyer.'

'The marriage application is in; you need a ring.'

It wasn't just that. The meeting with the lawyer could very well end them, Carter knew.

Grace was proud, and he wanted her to have something. Something she could sell. And this was the best he could come up with.

He flicked on the lights, hoping that would help. But now he could see the pucker of her areolae, so he moved his gaze up and saw that plump mouth.

'What one would you choose?' She met his eyes then. 'After all, I'll be returning it to you in twelve months.'

'You get to keep it.'

'Why?'

'Gifts,' he said. 'Jonathon will explain."

He watched her fingers hover over the diamonds, the rubies, as the lights caught the precious gems and they sparkled beguilingly. And then he watched her pause over a magnificent teardrop emerald. It was beautiful, yes—stunningly so. But if she was thinking of her future…

'The diamond next to it is exceptional.' He pointed to it, several carats worth, and the one she was supposed to select. The one every other bride marrying for money would swoop on like a magpie.

'It's too big,' Grace said, then frowned, because of course the emerald was even bigger, yet just so gorgeous. 'Anyway, we're not for ever,' she said.

And, selection made, she took out the emerald ring, looking at the beautiful stone set in white gold, and felt as if she'd been struck in the throat.

She had never thought that selecting a ring for a fake engagement would cause her heart to implode—that she might have to keep her head down so he wouldn't see the tears that filled her eyes as she examined it.

'It's beautiful.'

Her voice was a tremble as she looked at the stone, at the flashes of yellow and green, like tiny fireflies, and for a second, she was transported back to a time when all she had wanted was one night. Deep in the jungle she'd felt on the edge of for ever, utterly alone with him and without agenda.

'I love it.' She told him the truth. 'I'll want to keep it for ever.'

'Don't get romantic,' he told her.

'No, but I'm allowed to adore it.'

'Grace, you're going to sell it. For now, though, if it's too big it can be resized,' he said, taking her hand.

He looked at the gorgeous ring, slipping a little on her slender finger, and he felt something deep inside. What he felt, he didn't quite know—but it was unwelcome.

Was it the painful thaw of black ice cracking?

It wasn't desire, yet it was laced with it...

He did not want to care.

Not too much.

He snapped the box closed. 'If you change your mind, they're not going back till tomorrow.'

'I shan't change my mind.'

Grace wouldn't. She was under the covers with one hand out, admiring her ring, when he came back from the safe. But when he climbed into bed she turned and faced him, ran a newly bejewelled hand along his smooth jaw. It was almost the same Carter she'd met that first day.

'I forgot how good-looking you are,' she said, and her honesty surprised her—it was as if she'd forgotten how to be shy.

'You prefer me shaved?'

'No,' she admitted. 'I just…forget sometimes.'

She examined his features and they were as gorgeous as they had been that very first day, and yet then it would have been rude to fully stare, or to reach out and touch.

'The first time I saw you…' she smiled a slow, satisfied smile '… I thought I was dreaming.'

'Really?'

She nodded. 'I mean it. I thought you were part of my dream. I had no idea where I was. Bear in my mind I couldn't hear a thing. I thought it was a very nice, almost inappropriate dream.'

He smiled. 'The first time I saw you I thought of Sleeping Beauty.'

'Liar.'

'No.' He pushed her damp hair from her face. 'Well, actually I thought, when I saw your passport on the floor, that you were not my problem.'

'I'm *not* your problem,' Grace said.

Possibly, she pondered, that was the beauty of them. They weren't each other's problem—instead they were each other's solution.

Maybe that was why it felt so right.

It was a nice thought to fall asleep on.

Grace woke up alone.

Well, she heard the door close and realised there were to be no morning kisses goodbye or…

Staring at her ring, she told herself she was being ridiculous, and rang for tea and pancakes. And then, as she always did, she took a breath before checking her messages.

None from the care home.

Phew.

And just as she was about to call Carter, ask what the plans were for tonight, her phone rang and it was the Ms Hill she'd heard mentioned several times.

'The stylist is booked for midday, but I've left hair and make-up till five, given you're meeting Carter at seven.'

She gave Grace the location.

'He's not coming back here?'

'No…' She seemed to be checking. 'Seven p.m. reception. The car will be booked for six-forty-five.'

'Thanks so much,' Grace said. 'Do you know…?' She stopped. 'Actually, I'll call him myself.'

'Excuse me?'

'I'll call Carter.'

'If you need Mr Bennett for any reason, then you can contact me.'

'I meant for a personal reason.'

'You can contact me any time.'

Grace felt her lips stretch into an incredulous smile. 'What about in an emergency?'

'If I deem it an emergency, I'll be certain to pass it on.'

Oh, my gosh!

Grace wanted to be Ms Hill, she truly did—even if she was cross.

So cross that the moment the call ended she called Carter directly—just because she could.

Or, she thought she could—'How can I help you, Grace?' Ms Hill answered.

Grace gritted her teeth. 'Is it very formal tonight?'

'I've given Mr Bennett's schedule to the stylist. She'll be able to direct you.'

'Thank you.'

It was unexpected, and it jolted. She'd thought she had his number, had slept with him last night, and now she had to go through his PA in England to find out what to wear for dinner...

Her perfect dream makeover day was—oddly—not quite so.

'Wow!' Grace said, because her hair had been straightened and looked like silk.

Then she was shown it from the back, and if she hadn't known, then she'd never have guessed it was her own reflection.

She glanced at her toenails which were no longer painted a faded coral—in fact they were back to their natural colour, only buffed and polished, as were her fingernails.

It really was like a theatrical production, with a break for light snacks before wardrobe was called.

Grace felt an odd pang of disappointment at the underwear selection. It was gorgeous, she was told. Sheer and so barely there...

She felt barely there.

She felt as if she'd been dipped in ink stain remover as she tried on endless clothes.

There were pale dresses, cool linen suits and beautiful shoes. But for someone who had lived the last two years in yoga pants or cargo pants, it was a little less thrilling than she'd imagined.

'Beige?' She flicked through the dresses. 'Grey?'

They were 'wheaten' and 'pewter', apparently, but there was just no colour anywhere, save for a very pale blue trouser suit—so pale it was almost off the spectrum.

'We're just building a basic wardrobe,' the stylist informed her. 'You can then add your own signature.'

So she chose suitable outfits for day—cool linen trousers and light jackets—and then her hand hovered over an oatmeal linen smock with spaghetti straps that would be gorgeous to throw on after the pool.

'That's stunning,' the assistant said, but then Grace looked at the layering, the beauty of the garment and the designer tag, and hastily put it back. No, that was *not* a dress to throw on when she was damp from the pool. Instead she turned her attention to the evening wear.

Ms Hill had indeed given the stylist Carter's schedule—business dinners, performing arts, restaurants... She even had to choose outfits to wear should she have to join him in the Middle East...

And as she tried on clothes she felt as if she were dressing for a man she didn't know—certainly not a man who didn't seem bothered by shorts and tatty tops or bright red sarongs... a man who stood so quiet and still watching the dawn break... nor one who handed her a lilac flower.

Finally, it was time for make-up.

Or rather for her foundation to be matched and lessons on application to be had.

She rather failed with eyeliner and looked at the gorgeous eyes of the beautician, wanting them!

'How do I do wings?'

'You don't,' she was sharply told. 'If you want a smoky-eyed look then it is better to call us.'

The car was there, as arranged, and it took her to another very nice hotel. She sat in Reception, nervous and unsure, leaping on her phone with relief when it rang with a video call.

'Violet!' Grace quickly changed hands so that she held the phone with her left one, so as to hide the enormous ring.

'Oh, my God!' Violet said, when she saw her. 'Grace, you look....'

'I just got my hair done.'

'You've had *everything* done! Where are you?'

'Waiting in Reception at some fancy hotel,' Grace admitted, but then played it down. 'I'm just going for drinks…'

'With…?' Violet asked eagerly. 'Come on, Grace.'

'Some guy I met on the tour.'

'You look incredible!'

Violet was excited, and Grace wished it were a little more infectious.

'Different,' Violet said, cocking her blonde head to the side. 'But amazing. I hardly recognise you.'

Neither did Carter for a moment.

Her curls were gone, swept in a slick chignon, and he'd never noticed Grace's excellent posture before.

Correction. He'd examined her spine in detail, but he wasn't thinking about that now. Just her legs, long and slim in heels, nicely toned calves…

The dress was…well, a dress. But to his surprise he missed the curls.

And further to his surprise was the fact he'd noticed.

'Grace.'

She looked over, and as always her smile was more than her mouth. She smiled with her body, stepped towards him and raised an arm—a whole welcome with a smile.

'They're already here,' he told her.

He handed his laptop and the precious blueprints that barely left his side over to the concierge, and asked him to lock them away.

Grace was waiting for him to comment—on her make-up, her hair, anything—but he didn't.

'Simi and Tengku,' he told her as they walked through.

'I tried to call you…'

'Ms Hill said.'

She stopped—just stopped walking. And that was another thing Grace did—another damn thing he'd noticed.

'If you ever do that on the underground in London you'll cause a pile-up.'

He saw her angry face beneath the perfect make-up and found he missed her freckles too.

'Grace, I don't take personal calls at work.'

'Ever?'

'Never.' There was no one important enough—he very deliberately kept it that way. 'Now, are we going to do this?'

'Yes.'

Grace nodded, wondering how to 'do this'—how to sleep with someone at night who was completely unavailable by day.

A man who didn't even notice the effort you'd made.

Even if he'd paid for it.

A man who, without effort, always made her smile.

'Simi, Tengku—this is Grace.'

'It's lovely to meet you.'

They were surely *not* in the top one hundred most beautiful people—they were portly and happy and normal… Well, apart from their surroundings and their wealth.

And as she took a seat, and Tengku tucked a napkin under his ribs, she caught Carter's eyes.

Got you! said his smile.

He very possibly had.

CHAPTER NINE

'CARTER, LOOK!'

It was his father calling to him again, and he turned, saw Hugo looking back at him. Only it was Grace carrying him into the jungle rather than his mother.

And it couldn't be his father calling out, Carter realised, because his father lay face-down in the water with his arms spread out.

Or was that Grace floating?

His eyes snapped open. He was unsure for a moment if he'd shouted out, but presumably not, given that Grace lay wrapped around him like bindweed.

He'd have to remind her again that he liked space in bed.

Especially if they were going to be doing this for a year!

Carter gulped in air, went to move her so he could sit on the edge of the bed, catch his breath and drink water. But his heart was slowing down, and her skin was warm and alive.

'Carter…?'

She lifted her head from his chest, and it was like the first time they'd met. For her eyes were open, yet she was more asleep than awake. 'What time…?'

'Early,' he said. 'Go back to sleep.'

He felt the weight of her head as it sank back down on his chest, and the tickle of her hair on his chin didn't even irritate him.

He'd thought the nightmares had returned because he'd

been in Borneo, yet he'd been back in KL for more than a week.

It was the teething ring unsettling him, he was certain, even in the dressing room and behind the solid walls of the hotel safe, it was pulsing like a radioactive alarm.

It was the anniversary of his family's deaths coming up, and he was seriously considering once more asking Arif to return it to the jungle.

He'd been too sideswiped at the time to think straight, and had let him load it onto the boat.

No, he would not be asking.

He would be telling.

In fact, he might call Arif and ask to meet him. Give it back to him and tell him to damn well return it to where it belonged.

Arif's father might have saved his life, but he was surely no longer beholden? He'd taken that week off work to look into things, and now—not that Arif knew it—he was possibly going to marry a woman when he didn't want...

Except he did want.

Constantly.

Usually, sex was a like a prescription for him.

To be taken as required.

Necessary, pleasurable, it relieved an ache, took care of a basic need.

Now he was seeking her needs, turned on by her climaxing, feeling her at times holding back...

Her thigh was over his now, her hand low on the side of his stomach, and he was hardening as if he were reaching for her, almost willing her hand to slip further down. Wanting her to react to his desire as his more vigilant lovers would have...

And yet he liked the chase, the flirtation, and so he lay there, feeling her even breathing, her inhalations so deep she was on the edge of a gentle snore. The horror of the nightmare had faded, it was nice to simply lie there and hold her...

* * *

'Carter?'

He frowned at Grace's groggy voice.

'We've overslept.'

'No.'

He turned to the clock. He never overslept. And neither did he fall back to sleep after a nightmare.

It was a bit of a rush.

Grace forgot to wear a shower cap and, no matter how brilliant the hairdresser, there wasn't a product invented that could tame her curls. To see the lawyer, she settled for the very pale powder blue trouser suit, and pulled on the awful underwear—a little bandeau bra thing that she had to put on over her head, and knickers that were sheer enough not to be noticed whatever she wore. The unfortunate pay-off being they came up close to her belly button.

God, she'd have preferred red velvet and suspenders, she thought, or at least she'd thought Carter would have preferred that.

She added a little cami, and then the suit, and slipped on some heels.

'We need to get a move on, Grace,' Carter warned.

'Then lucky for you I'm ready.'

'Back to curls?'

He looked at them, all pinned up, and was about to say he preferred them—though that wasn't his place. Nor was it for him to say that he missed her red sarong, and the dusky pink top, the coral on her nails.

Grace had said she was sorting out her clothes and her hair herself, and who was he to debate her choices? Even so, he did comment on her tension.

'Are you okay?' he checked. 'You look nervous.'

'Well, it's not every day you sign a contract for two million dollars.'

'It's just the NDA today.' He waved away her concerns. 'Then he'll walk us through the prenup. He might get a bit personal, but it's necessary.'

'Why?'

'Because…' he tried to keep his voice patient '…we are going to be marrying, and divorcing, and presumably sleeping together.' He was not going to startle her before they even got out of the stalls. 'Let's get some breakfast.'

They headed up to the restaurant, and as they were led to their table Grace looked at all the busyness and inhaled the scents. He seemed so at ease here.

'I don't know where to start…' she admitted, eyeing the gorgeous buffet.

As it turned out, his schedule was too tight for a buffet, and she was back to looking at menus again.

'I just want toast,' she said.

'No coffee?' He frowned.

'Tea,' Grace said. She was a bundle of nerves as it was.

She ordered exactly that when the waiter came.

Carter, though, appeared starving—from all the sex they *hadn't* had this morning? He ordered *nasi lemak*, and she wondered how he had the stomach for such a spicy dish so early, and how he had not even a hint of the nerves she was feeling…

'We're having dinner with them after,' he told her.

'Who?'

'Jonathon and Ruth—my lawyer and his wife.'

She shook her head as if to clear it. 'Seriously?'

Carter saw her shaking hand as she attempted to add marmalade to her toast, and knew he needed this to work.

'He might ask about your father,' he warned her.

'He can ask,' Grace said. 'I have no idea where he is.'

'You know once this hits the news there's a chance he'll get in touch?'

'I don't care.' She shrugged. 'Honestly, I have nothing to say to him.' She poured some tea. 'I last saw him in the interval of a pantomime. He popped out to get a drink.'

Carter waited. 'And…?' he prompted.

'That was it.' She added sugar to her tea. 'I must be boring company, because I haven't seen him since. I don't care if he gets in touch, or pleads for money, or tells whatever lie he comes up with…'

'So, I don't have to ask his permission?'

'No!' she replied hotly, and then looked up as if she'd realised it was she who had missed a small joke.

This time she didn't smile back.

'Excuse me for a moment,' Carter said.

He didn't explain where he was going and neither did she ask. There were several meeting rooms off the corridor just down from the restaurant—places to withdraw for private discussions or to toast success…

Jonathon was already there, of course.

A gleaming desk was all set up—there was a delicate floral arrangement as well as a jug of iced tea and pretty glasses, water and notepads. But for all the luxury and creature comforts he knew that to Grace this would appear as clinical as a hospital… Or rather that the topics about to be discussed would not be softened by the surroundings.

'Ready when you are,' Jonathan informed him.

Despite his somewhat genial appearance, Carter knew that Jonathon's mood could and often did quickly change. He had been on his side since he'd come out of the jungle, an orphaned eight-year-old with a fortune ripe to be misused by others.

'We can expect some pushback from Benedict, but—'

Carter cut in. 'I want you to listen to Grace.'

'Of course,' Jonathon said. 'But we shan't budge—'

'No.' Carter interrupted again. 'She has no one representing her.'

'Excellent.'

'There's a small possibility she's pregnant—'

Now Jonathon stopped leafing through the preliminary draft. Perhaps he saw Carter's grim expression, because it was Jonathon who interrupted now. 'Should the situation arise, it will be dealt with.'

'Go easy,' Carter warned.

'I don't play softball.'

'Just…' Carter made a gesture with his hand. 'I want the marriage to go ahead. There's a lot at stake.'

'Oh, I'm well aware,' Jonathon warned—and Carter knew he wasn't referring to the land, more his client's vast fortune. 'You need this to be watertight.'

'And I'm telling you to tread gently.'

Those were his instructions.

It was for the sake of his grandfather's legacy that he was reining Jonathon in, Carter told himself as he walked back to where Grace sat.

'Ready?'

She nodded and stood, and he watched as she blew out a breath.

Perhaps, he considered as they walked towards the meeting room, Grace was right. He should have chosen someone more suited to a world of convenient marriages.

They took their seats across from Jonathon and, as always, Carter started to leaf through the documents at his place. Grace sat ramrod-straight.

'It's fairly straightforward…' Jonathon kicked things off. 'Anything you don't understand, feel free to interject. First things first, though: we can't proceed without an NDA.' He glanced to Carter. 'Has this already been raised?'

'It has.'

* * *

For something 'straightforward', Grace soon found out the devastating price she would pay if she broke her silence. And after reading through the first of the contracts she broke her silence now.

'All proceeds? A percentage of my future earnings? You know I'm struggling…' She shook her head and stared aghast at Carter. 'I've already told you I don't want anyone to know.'

Carter stared ahead. He knew he was an utter bastard in negotiations but he was trying to hold back, so he left Jonathon to do the talking.

'If you don't divulge, then there's no issue.'

On and on Jonathon went, explaining that things could go no further until the document was signed. That it was to protect them both. That Carter's previous partner had taken out a two-page spread in a magazine…

'So?' Grace asked. 'I'm not carrying the can for something one of his many exes might have done.'

Carter glanced at Jonathon, who'd clearly expected the NDA to be a trifling matter. In truth, so too had Carter—he'd thought this was the easy part!

'Indefinitely?' she checked, the reality of that single word dawning. 'I can *never* tell anyone?'

'It's quite standard,' Jonathon said.

Not to Grace.

Oh, it wasn't the wedding, nor even the year they would spend together.

It was after.

Grace caught a tiny glimpse of the future then—a life after Carter, all her problems seemingly solved. But he'd be gone.

She pushed the chair back and stood. 'I'd like to take a break, please.'

She felt a little giddy, and the dim lights of the corridor did nothing to soothe her—they annoyed her, in fact.

She took the elevator down, and even if Kuala Lumpur

wasn't the best place for cool air, it was so vibrant, so alive, it was still a relief to be out of the formal surroundings, to watch the busy city, the people, the cars, the noise…

'Grace.' Carter had come out. 'What the hell? If you're going to storm out over every clause this is going to be a very long day.'

Her response was silence.

'There has to be something in writing to ensure this remains between us, but I'm hardly really going to go after your wages.'

'Violet's been there for me every step of the way—and, believe me, given how I doubted her, it has nothing to do with *obligation*,' she sneered. 'That ran out a long time ago… It's about friendship…love.'

She looked at Carter then, a man who actively turned his back on the things she treasured the most.

'You couldn't begin to understand,' she said.

For someone who tried to be kind, she was possibly being mean now—but, hell, this morning had made her so.

'I know you lost your family, and I can't ever fathom how dreadful it was to lose them all in an instant.'

She stared at his granite features, saw now why he preferred the cold world of business, the towers, the noise.

'But I lose my mother a little bit more each day, and my friend is there for me. A year or so from now you'll be gone…' Grace said.

Her voice trailed off as she glimpsed the devastation she might feel and, frantically not wanting him to see, she reminded herself that emotions—at least deep ones—were not, nor ever could be allowed.

'What do I tell her?'

'Just say that we didn't work out.'

'Please…' She gave a mirthless laugh. 'That's not going to work with Violet…'

'Then it's up to you to make it work,' he warned. 'This isn't a game, or about placating friends.'

Grace swallowed as she suddenly got a front seat row to his ruthless edge as he very succinctly reminded her that this was a business arrangement, not a cosy deal.

She thought of her mother, reminded herself that was the real reason she was even sitting down to sign a contract. And yet there was a lump building in her throat.

Pulling herself away from the wall, Grace simply refused to let him see how deeply this was affecting her. 'Oh, well…' she shrugged '…at least I'll be rich.'

'And Grace…?' He called her back, waited till she'd turned around. 'If we do somehow manage to get past the NDA without you melting down, then we move on to the marriage contract. That won't be getting signed today…'

'What does that mean?'

'It means there's no need to argue every point or storm out.' His eyes never left her face, and his voice was curt. 'Some personal details will be raised—don't get all offended, just make a note on the paper provided and we can discuss it between ourselves later.'

'Fine.'

'Grace, I told you right from the start you couldn't tell Violet.'

'I thought that meant while we were married.' She looked at him. 'I don't even know if I'll ever want tell her, but maybe in time…'

Carter arched his neck when she'd gone.

He loved the sounds of a city—any city. Usually they drowned out the thoughts in his head. But now all he could see was the sight of her strained features. And, no matter how self-sufficient *he* chose to be, he knew that Grace was close to her friend and that they relied on each other. He wasn't used to that. Not just for himself…all the women he generally dated would know the score.

This was a business decision.

He thought of Arif, impatient at eight, wanting to know what had happened to his friend.

Of Bashim telling him to give it time.

And, no, he'd never been ready to talk to his friend…

Yet here he was, taking that right away from Grace.

Damn.

He took the elevator up, walked back into the meeting room where she sat, taking a long drink of water. And the ridiculous thing was that he missed her small smile when he entered. The tiny moments of eye contact they had started to share. The feeling they were both in this together.

It would seem that he had the business meeting he wanted.

'Are we ready to resume?' Jonathon checked.

'Sure,' Grace responded.

'It's a standard agreement,' Jonathon started. 'And not just for your own protection. If the press or Benedict attempt to approach your family or friends, this ensures they don't know anything.'

'I understand,' Grace responded, her voice almost a monotone, but she frowned when Carter spoke.

'Add an exclusion…' He turned to Grace, and knew he didn't even need to ask if she trusted her friend—she'd already told him her life's regret was a brief moment in time when she'd doubted her, simply to save herself from the reality of facing her mother's diagnosis. 'What's Violet's surname?'

'Lewis.'

Jonathon was less than willing, pointing out that Violet would need to agree to sign her own NDA, that there was no guarantee otherwise.

'Violet Lews is to be excluded at Grace's discretion.'

'The consequences remain,' Jonathon warned.

She must really trust her friend, Carter thought as finally, one hour and forty-seven minutes after the meeting had commenced, Grace picked up her pen.

Now came the hard part.

He glanced up as Jonathon took his jacket off.

It would be some considerable time till they were alone...

If Grace lasted that long!

CHAPTER TEN

'WELL DONE,' CARTER SAID, steering Grace, who was almost fizzing with silent anger, to the elevator.

It was close to midnight as they left the restaurant, having had a long dinner with Jonathon and his wife.

Somehow she had held her temper and made notes throughout the long meeting. Somehow she had not stood up and walked out as extremely intimate details had been discussed. Then, the audacity of having to sit through dinner!

No room full of candles was going to fix this, she thought, as they stepped into the suite.

'DNA!' She was as close to slapping another person as she had ever come as—now they were in private—she raised the points that had hurt the most. 'I thought the NDA was bad enough, but...' She looked at him in abject fury. 'You laughed when he said you'd insist on a DNA test and I had to just sit there.'

'I did not laugh,' Carter corrected. 'I smothered a smile.' He took her by the arms. 'Grace, he was just saying that if you are already pregnant...'

She finished for him. 'You'd demand a DNA test.'

'Did you want me to tell Jonathon that you were a virgin? That we both got carried away? Because I could have—and do you know what? He would have still insisted the DNA clause remained.'

'In case I spend the next few weeks frantically trying to

get pregnant so I can blame it on you because you're such a big shot?'

'Something like that,' he said.

He moved away and punched out two headache tablets, adding another and swallowing them down with a drink that she was sure wasn't the one recommended on the packet.

'Then we had to sit through dinner afterwards...as if I hadn't just been insulted.'

'He's just doing his job.'

She kicked off her shoes. 'I am *so* not suited for this.'

Then she took off the horrible pale jacket, and the trousers, too, and decided she wasn't suited to suits either.

'I agree,' Carter nodded, tearing off his tie as if it were choking him, and his jacket and shoes too, and then his socks. He lay back on the bed. 'Believe it or not, it's your unsuitability for this that makes marriage doable for me.'

'I don't get it.'

'Grace, I take my dates to the theatre, so I don't have to talk to them. I can't imagine getting past time in the jungle with any of them, let alone them agreeing to a wedding there, without exclusive photos and a freaking string quartet and white chairs with bows, a few celebrity guests...' He covered his eyes with the back of his arm and groaned. 'At least you just want money and a peaceful life.'

Grace was almost terribly pleased he was deep in migraine land, so that he could not see her awkward swallow.

Even as she denied it, even as she ignored it and told all the thoughts to go away, as she sat on the bed and looked over to where he lay she knew the reason for the sudden clarity that had struck her when she'd agreed to this madness. How the impossible decision had been made so easily...

She was more than a bit crazy about him.

Fascinated by him, really.

Trust her to go and fall for the one man who actually *was* an island...well, at least most of the time. Because now he pulled down his forearm and gave her a half-grimace and a half-smile that almost felt like an apology.

'Seriously, I know it was hell in there.'

'I hated it,' she admitted, still appalled at all that had been discussed, right down to those awful 'discreet affair' clauses. 'All of it.'

There were so many things that had upset her today, Grace thought as she headed into the bathroom. Finally alone, she took the clips from her hair and then washed the make-up off her face.

She was too weary to take off her cami, let alone her colourless underwear, and she just stared in the mirror and didn't know who she was any more.

By night she felt safe in the decision she was making. Making love with Carter, she felt giddy with desire, safe to take risks, to watch in the mirror as he took her as if seeing herself come to life.

Right now, she didn't even know if she liked him.

But that question faded when she saw him dozing on the bed. He was why she was here—not that she was going to admit that. And she really was the luckiest—not for ever, of course, but for now. She felt lucky to be able to climb up onto the bed, to take a little of his *don't give a damn* attitude and curl into him.

'What are you doing?' he asked, pulling away from her touch as she laid her head on his chest.

'Checking there's actually a heart in there.' She felt his half-laugh. 'I don't like Jonathon. I don't get why we had to sit down to dinner and make small talk with him and his wife...'

'Because...' he said. But, as was so often the case with Carter, he didn't elaborate. He tried to peel her off him. 'Get undressed and get some sleep.'

'I don't want to.' She was too tired even to move, but after a day of having details discussed such as their having no love, no involvement afterwards, no expectations, she could not turn her mind off. 'He seems *very* familiar with your private life.'

'Of course he is. About ten years ago there was a lawsuit about twins. I think the woman was just hoping I'd pay up, but Jonathon shot that down very quickly. Look it up.'

'I already have.'

'Then you'll know about the guy I supposedly dated?'

'Yes.'

'An attempt to bribe me. Look, Jonathon knows I don't want a relationship, he knows that I'm straight, and that my family are useless. I don't have to repeatedly tell him that I never want kids, and he knows without asking that I don't have unprotected sex. So, yes, it's probably a surprise to him that I'm suddenly engaged and forgot to be cautious.' He gave her shoulder a squeeze. 'Don't take it all so personally.'

'Oh, it feels personal. But why did we have dinner with them?'

'Aren't you supposed to be calling the care home? Wasn't that meeting today? It's almost four in London.'

'You're like one of those time zone walls at the stock exchange...' Grace grumbled, half relieved he'd reminded her, but also certain he was trying to avoid the discussion. Still, if she wanted to catch the manager before she went home then now was the time to call.

Peeling herself from the reprieve of his arms, she sat up on the edge of the bed.

His arm had gone back across his head, and she was certain he was dozing—anyway, she doubted her mother's care plan meeting was high on his list of priorities.

'Maggie!' She was relieved to reach the manager, especially when she heard it was all good news. 'They're reducing her medication?' Grace blinked, thrilled to hear that her sedation was being cut back.

And not only that...

'That's so sweet of her,' she said, when she heard that Violet had been bringing in a chocolate éclair each Sunday, just dropping it off at Reception so as not to upset her mother.

Oh, and she needed new lenses for her glasses... Grace chose not to ask about her hearing tests—not just yet. Anyway, there was something more that had been worrying her.

'Is she still asking for me all the time?'

The response was one she hadn't expected, and she wished—oh, how she wished—she'd taken the call in the lounge, or some other area of the opulent suite.

It was ridiculous to get good news and want to cry.

Carter knew damn well he'd changed the subject rather than answer her question, but behind his forearm he frowned at Grace's long silence in response to whatever the answer to her last question had been.

'Oh,' she finally said. 'That's good... I guess.'

'Everything okay?' he checked when she'd ended the call.

'Yes,' she said, just a little too brightly.

Carter removed his arm and looked to where she sat, her back to him.

'Are you sure?' Carter checked.

'Just leave it.'

'Grace?'

'She's stopped asking for me. Apparently, she refers to me being at school, but...' She swallowed. 'It's good news, I guess.' Then her voice changed from falsely upbeat to hollow. 'I didn't expect it.'

For a moment the false wall she'd put up had nothing to support it, and he reached out, completely on instinct, to put a hand on her shoulder. But she brushed it off.

'I don't want to talk about it.'

'You can.'

'I don't want to.'

'Come here,' he said again, and pulled her, tense and yet yielding, back into his arms. Only it wasn't the same relaxed space as before. 'She probably—'

'Carter,' she interrupted. 'It hurts to talk about it.'

'I know.'

'So can we change the subject? Like you did when I asked why we had to have dinner with your lawyer?'

She lay there.

'If I get my own, will you sit through a chummy dinner with them?'

'No.' He gave a soft laugh, realising now how odd it must have seemed. 'Jonathon does a lot for me.'

'You pay him to.'

'Not just that.'

He loathed sharing anything personal, but he'd just asked for the same from her. More, he'd asked her to sit through dinner with two people who were not only clearly on his side, but actively suspicious of her.

'I don't expect you to get it, but they have both looked out for me. A lot.'

'How?'

He swallowed before he told her something very few knew—and it had nothing to with the fact she'd signed the NDA.

That wasn't even a thought in his head.

More, it felt right to reveal it.

'I lived with them for a couple of months while it was decided where I'd end up. Jonathon wanted to be sure I had a say—well, of sorts. I wasn't talking then.'

'At all?'

'Not much. I could hear, though.' He gave her shoulder a squeeze, making another little joke, even if the topic wasn't funny. But it seemed they had this new language they shared, because she looked up briefly and smiled.

'What did you hear?' Grace asked.

* * *

Her head went back to his chest, her eyes open as she listened. Usually she'd close her eyes to picture things. Only now she needed every detail—how one hand held her arm, and the other found her fingers and toyed with her ring as he spoke.

'My uncle was prepared to have me,' he said.

'Benedict's father?'

'Yep,' he said. 'Well, he wanted to get his hands on my parents' money. We'd be lying in a cheap motel now if he'd got his hands on it.'

Grace found that she was smiling, wishing she was in a motel with him for gorgeous, uncomplicated sex. Pull-up-the-car-and-get-a-room sex. And she found that she blinked in shock at her own thoughts, especially when they were discussing something so serious.

'What's funny?' he asked, and it dawned on her that he, too, was aware of even her tiniest movement.

'Us in a motel.'

'What about it?'

'You were talking about your uncle…' She nudged him, knowing he would happily stay off track and wanting to know more.

'Jonathon threatened my uncle with an exposé, so he soon pulled out. Really, you can see where Benedict gets it from. Then there was my grandfather… He was eccentric, at best, and grieving.'

He fell silent for a moment, and she watched his finger hover over the stone of her ring.

'As well as that, I didn't want to go back to Borneo—it was a couple of years before I did. And it was Jonathon and his wife who stepped up.'

'So they took you in?'

'They did. And I think I could have stayed for longer. But then my aunt in New York decided she needed to be seen doing her part.'

He told her about his mother's sister, and how she really wasn't 'mommy material'.

'That lasted a couple of years before she shipped me off, back to boarding school in England. Jonathon's always looked out for me and, as expensive as he is, he has never once taken advantage…'

'Do I have to like them now?'

'No, just understand where they're coming from.' He played with the edge of her cami. 'Get undressed?' he suggested.

'I honestly can't be bothered.' She liked being sad in his arms.

'Nor can I,' he admitted. 'I'm sorry you're upset about your mum.'

'Thank you.'

She knew he'd possibly shared with an agenda, but it was a nice agenda—to give a bit of himself, to know her some more.

'I've been worried the whole time I've been away that she'll think I've forgotten her. I never gave much thought to her forgetting me.' She took a breath, but it shuddered. It was five staccato gasps just to get one breath in, and it was the closest to crying she'd come. 'I don't want to be forgotten…'

'I know.'

There was something else that had upset her during the discussions today. 'Why are you having a vasectomy?' she asked.

'I've been meaning to.' She watched as his hand moved to his crotch, as if to protect it, but then moved away. 'Though it didn't seem urgent until the other night.'

She lay there, trying to tell herself it was ridiculous to be upset about something so sensible—something he clearly wanted. Or rather to think about babies he didn't want, and certainly not with her.

He picked up her hand and looked at her ring and she knew he was about to change the subject again—but at least she understood why. It was too painful for him to recall.

'Why the hell did you choose this one?'

'Fireflies.' Grace smiled and let him talk about nothing rather than desperate hurt. 'When we were just a one-night stand...'

'Seriously?'

'Mmm...' she said. 'Then you had to go and propose, and bring in lawyers and stylists.'

'I thought you wanted stylists?'

'Not any more,' Grace admitted. 'I miss us.'

'Do you?'

He looked down at her pale leg, lying over his. 'I miss your coral toenails,' he told her.

'So do I.' She liked the *thud-thud* of his heart and how neither of them moved. 'I love coral... I love colour.'

Carter frowned, unsure how to respond. If he *should* respond!

'So why all the...?'

'They suggested I start with a neutral palette and then add my own signature.'

'You already have your own signature.'

'I don't think so?'

'Oh, you do,' he assured her. 'Well, you did.'

'What is it?'

'Sunset colours. Sunrise, maybe. I don't know... But it's not neutral...' He actually gritted his jaw. 'You're more vibrant... a bit...'

Careful Carter, he thought.

'Dishevelled...'

'I was dishevelled when we met because I'd been travelling and was asleep. Then the jungle...'

'I like your curls,' he said. 'And how your top falls off your shoulder. Always...' he stuck with his chosen word '...dishevelled.'

'Slatternly, as my mother would say.'

He liked her soft laugh.

'Though not any more. Even my underwear is sensible.'

He frowned, pulling at her cami, stretching his hand around her back.

'It's a bandeau,' she said. 'No hooks.'

He pulled her up onto his stomach, took off her cami and looked at the little strip of material, and her dark nipples all squashed by the fabric.

'Like a bank robber,' he said, and they laughed. 'I like these,' he said of the glossy knickers. He could see the darkness of her triangle of hair and tried to unfocus his eyes. 'You look naked.'

'I thought you'd be more into velvet and lace.'

'You so have the wrong impression of me,' he said. 'I am not really bothered by underwear...' He was almost too tired to speak now, so his words were sort of a drawl. 'More what's under the underwear.' Then he pushed her breasts together and changed his mind. 'You have the best breasts...'

He moved down to her invisible knickers and dusted her thighs with his hands. And then he pulled her head down.

He had never expected a kiss like this when they'd walked through the door. Certainly, he had not expected for all the tension that had built through the day to be erased by deep and real conversation. Nor, as he'd led her angrily from the restaurant, had he envisaged this slow intimate kiss. Their mouths were too tired to talk, their bodies almost too tired to move, but somehow he was in deep discovery, because his hands were peeling down the knickers she loathed.

'I hate them too,' he said, for they refused to tear.

There was something so inherently pleasurable watching her sensual nature emerge. 'I was worried they'd get rid of this,' he told her as he stroked her triangle of hair through the flimsy fabric.

'They suggested it...' She blushed so deeply the colour speckled her neck. 'I refused.'

'Good.'

'Get what *you* want, Grace...'

'I want this.'

* * *

Perhaps he heard the urgent note, because Carter tried again to tear at the fabric, but they were better designed than that, and Grace didn't want to get off his sexy hot body.

He lifted her bottom, brought her towards him and raised his head, and she held the bedhead as he tore the fabric with his teeth.

It was the sexiest thing she'd ever felt…his head on her stomach, his hand on her bottom and the tearing of her knickers.

'There,' he said.

It was a very slow start, because he'd managed only to rip the fabric to the edge of her thigh, then it was back up again for another nibble from his teeth.

He slid them down one thigh and didn't go back down. He slipped a little lower and tasted her. It was something she had never thought she could enjoy. In truth, as she closed her eyes, she was too tense to know if she actually did.

'Grace…' He probed and he licked and he relished, and she felt herself pressing down a little for more of the bliss. 'Give me a little climax…'

'I can't—'

Famous last words, because he pulled her down onto him till she was gripping the bedhead and fighting not to cry out, such bliss he delivered with his mouth.

'That's it…' he said, stroking her bottom with his hand as he stroked her with his tongue. She gave him a little, a flicker of orgasm, but he knew as she lifted from him, that she held back a lot.

He sat her down on his thighs, felt her hand close around him, and not shyly, just so blissfully.

They were both panting, both turning the other on, but with more than just touch—they were crossing into each other's thoughts. 'Why did you smile when I said motel?' he asked and her flushed face darkened, yet she stroked him still.

'The thought of…' she shook her head.

'Go on?' he invited, deeply curious to hear more.

'The thought of wanting another so much that you simply have to stop the car...' she gave a half nervous laugh. 'Or meet in your lunch break...'

Carter had never wanted anyone in that way.

Yet he wanted her in that way now.

He reached for a condom and saw her eyes briefly close in frustration as he tore the wrapper.

If she had been anyone else it would have alerted him. He'd just been lectured by his lawyer, after all, to be very careful in the coming weeks. Instead it made him reckless. Their wants matched...this desire could not be contained.

'In a moment,' he said, and she nodded in weak relief.

And then it was Grace who knelt up and held his thick, unsheathed base, and together they watched her lower herself down onto him.

'God...' she moaned. Because he made her crave.

And she looked at him, half dressed, resting up on his forearms, as fascinated as she, she rested her hands on his chest and moved.

It was a dangerous, dangerous game and they both knew it, but they were in this together, this *folie à deux*, this shared madness, and she felt for the first time in her life completely free.

And also looked after, because he nodded and said, 'I won't come,'

He gave her his word, and with it she had permission to move again.

He stroked her breasts, pinched them, and he stroked her stomach, then round to her bottom. He didn't guide her, just inflamed her. He stroked her thighs and then, when she bit her lip, he thrust up into her, and she could not believe his control. How he could lie there and thrust and observe.

'Carter...'

She was holding the bedhead and moaning loudly, and then he started to pull her down hard, again and again, and Grace could hear herself shout. She was suddenly frantic, deeply orgasming and trying to lift off of him, yet he held her firm. Pulsing and making sounds she never had before. Then, when he could hold back no more, he took her by the hips and lifted her, and she watched him spill onto her. Breathless, she watched as his palm cupped her where she ached with the void he'd left.

He pulled her head down and they kissed as if it were their first time...wet, deep kisses. And in between he told her off... warned her not to play that game again...

'I won't.'

She could barely breathe. Her sex felt heavy and her stomach was still tight, as if unfulfilled. Yet she had never been more satisfied.

Carter wasn't faring so well. He rarely made mistakes, and certainly not the same one twice. Okay, he hadn't come inside her, but he was taking risks he never had before.

He wanted Grace more than he'd thought he was capable of.

But she deserved someone who could love her—completely.

He knew he was incapable of that.

Knew he had to pull back.

CHAPTER ELEVEN

IT WAS THE scent rather than the sound of Carter coming out of the shower that awoke Grace.

She knew his scents now.

He worked hard for his millions—or billions—and at the end of his working day there was just the last trace of bergamot on his jaw, and the masculine scent of Carter as he peeled off his shirt.

Possibly that was the one she loved the most.

Even so, the heady mixture of clean male, deodorant, and his sexy cologne was such a potent hit to the olfactory system that Grace was smiling even as she opened her eyes.

She thought of their lovemaking last night and lay watching as he pulled on his shirt and suit. He was clearly trying not to wake her, because he sat on a bedroom chair to put on his shoes, but then he must have seen her watching him.

'You're awake,' he said.

'It's early.' She frowned, peering at the time.

'I've got a flight at six.'

'You never said.'

'Didn't I?' He paused, then slipped on his second shoe. 'I thought I told you I had to go to Janana?'

He wasn't used to giving times and dates to anyone other than Ms Hill, who then did her usual magic with his schedule, but even so he was certain he'd mentioned it.

'The council's meeting. We have to make some last-minute changes to the plans.'

'For the palace?'

'That's right.'

It blew her mind that he was working on the restorations for some ancient palace while she was filling her days with designers and having her hair straightened, her nails or make-up done.

'When will you be back?' she asked.

'Depends.'

Carter moved his luggage out of the bedroom suite.

Seeing Grace stretch was like watching a flower open, or seeing how the giant ferns at the river edge unfurled.

But he didn't like the way his mind kept drifting to the river, and he kept waiting for boredom to kick in, for her to annoy him.

For her to stop creeping into his heart.

'You look tired,' she commented.

'No,' he disagreed, even though he knew he looked like hell. 'You've got Ms Hill's details. Any problems that Guest Services can't handle just call her.'

'Why can't I just call you? What if I—?'

'Grace.' He halted her right then and there. 'I've told you I don't take unscheduled calls during working hours. If there're any issues while I'm away then call Ms Hill, because you won't be able to get hold of me.'

She was tempted to ask, *Am I to tell Ms Hill if I get my period?* But she just lay back on the pillow, telling herself she wasn't even late yet.

He snapped on his heavy watch and frowned when he saw the time. 'There won't be any internet,' he told her. 'At least not if we go into the desert.'

'I thought it was just the palace?'

'There are some desert abodes he wants me to look at.' He shook his head. 'They look pre-biblical.'

'Seriously?'

'Apparently so. Sahir thinks they'll work better than a tent for his retreats.' He went to the safe to collect his passport. 'I'm going to—' He halted, suddenly feeling the silk of the pouch, then just grabbed his passport and turned around. 'It depends how quickly the council decide. I'd better go.'

'Sure.'

He picked up the plans and she pursed her lips as the man who had made such thorough love to her last night went to walk out through the door.

And then she reminded herself of his warning that they would never be close. She lay back on the pillow, feeling the tension in her own lips, holding back from telling him that she expected…

What *did* she expect? Grace chided herself.

Better than this!

And Grace was suddenly angry. She wasn't asking for love, or affection, just for him not to leave her feeling discarded.

Grace pulled on her robe and ventured out of the bedroom, saw the breakfast waiting for her. Bypassing it, she wrenched open the door.

'Carter…'

He was standing at the elevator when she walked down to him in her robe, still tying it.

'What?'

'You forgot something?'

He frowned. Had the audacity to check the inside pocket of his jacket.

'Back in the suite,' Grace said, her voice shaking with anger.

Because if he thought they could make love all night and then he did not even have to tell her his return date on the way out, then he could forget it.

'I get that it's a sham,' Grace told him, before the elevator doors closed, 'but if you don't want things to fall apart in the bedroom very quickly, then you'd better damn well learn how to say goodbye properly.'

'Poor Grace…' He had the audacity to smile. 'You want a kiss?'

'Not especially.' She stared at him. 'But I do expect basic manners.'

He made two kissing noises. 'See you soon, my darling…' he mocked, turning to go.

But possibly he then saw her furious eyes, because he bent his head and kissed her hard, forcing her lips apart, pulling her in.

'Better?'

'Screw you.'

'No,' he said. 'Neither of us are getting screwed, Grace. I have a long flight, and an important series of meetings. I haven't got the head space to play happy families in the morning, and don't expect me to come back bearing flowers.' He held up his hands in exasperation. 'What do you want? For me to pretend?'

'No.'

'To lie?'

'That's the last thing I want. I never want you to lie.'

She felt stupid. For pulling on the robe and running after him. And for not understanding that the intimacy they'd shared at night could be gone by morning. How, like a conjurer, he could whip away the cloth and leave everything standing.

Only the cloth was her heart, and she was starting to realise that she didn't know how to give it one moment and claim it back the next. Make love with him at night and be roommates by day.

'Grace…'

'It's fine. Go.'

Of course he did just that, and she stood there, tears filling her eyes.

She was scared that she was falling in love with a man incapable of love.

And worried too. Because while she wasn't technically late, her breasts hurt like hell. Or could that just be from sex?

She would go for a swim, Grace decided, slipping off her ring and looking at the pretty glinting lights. She'd go for a swim and then head to the Batu Caves. She would not spend the day dwelling on him…

That was all she was thinking as she went to pop her ring in the safe. Her hand brushed against something cool and, widening the door, she felt her mind leap at the brief distraction of a black silk pouch. She frowned as she lifted it, saw the fabric opening, and a glint of metal.

A silver bangle was her first thought as she slipped it out and weighed it in her hand. Only it was far too chunky and there was no hinge, no give in the gap that would allow it to slip on her wrist. It was heavy, too, and quite, quite beautiful.

So lost in the mystery of it, so relieved by the temporary reprieve of thoughts of Carter was she, that she didn't hear the door.

'What the hell do you think you're doing?'

She jumped at the whip of his voice and swung around. 'I just…'

She swallowed, unsure what to say. After all, she'd been caught snooping and it just wasn't like her.

'I don't know,' she admitted, trying to cram it back into the pouch. But she was all fingers and thumbs and so she just held the bangle out to him. 'I'm sorry.'

'Just put it back.'

It was as if he didn't even want to touch it.

'Christ, is there no privacy?' he demanded. 'I would *never* go through your things.'

'I wasn't…' Only that wasn't strictly true, and Grace knew it…

Seeing him so angry, so defensive, she guessed the bangle was meant for someone else.

'I hope she likes it…' She tossed him the damn thing but he made no attempt to catch it, just stood there as it fell to the floor.

As Grace headed to the bathroom, Carter stood, eyes closed.

He held the cold metal again for the first time since he'd handed it to his brother, fighting not to look down, to trace the scratches, doing all he could not to recall Hugo's trusting smile as he'd reached out to take it.

He'd let him down so badly…

Replacing it in the pouch, he returned it to the safe and then closed the door, breathing out as the lock bolted closed.

He was bizarrely conflicted. Because if it had been anyone else going through his property, touching something so private, he'd have had Security throw them out by now.

But he knew it had been a mistake, or just…

Some hotels were great for romance and sex but simply dreadful to have a row in, he thought. Because he could see her outline through the glass dividing door, see her back was turned. He knocked on the glass and she didn't need to turn. He could see her strained face in the huge mirrors.

'Grace…'

'I wasn't snooping…' Her voice was shaky. 'Well, clearly I was. But I didn't intend to. I just…' Her green eyes were anguished. 'I was putting my ring away and I saw the bangle…' She stopped. 'I saw the pouch.'

He smiled at her honest correction. 'I get it.' He nodded 'I overreacted.'

He could apologise for that and leave it there, but he knew more was required.

'It's not a bangle. It's a teething ring,' he told her. 'It was my brother's. It's been in the family for years. Polished up for each baby.'

'I'm so sorry.' Her eyes filled up and she looked at him, "It's lovely that you keep something of his…'

'No, Grace,' he corrected with a slight smile, 'I don't drag it around the world with me.' His smile paled. 'Ulat had it with him when he died.'

'Ulat?'

'Hugo. Ulat is what the locals call their babies for the first few months. He was just starting to be known as both. Arif goes back to the site each anniversary. It turned up last year and he gave it to me that night at the resort.'

That night.

'Was that why you were arguing?'

'In part.' He nodded. 'I told him he should have left it where it was.'

'You don't want it?'

'No.' He shook his head. 'I don't.'

He'd been in turmoil since it had been handed to him—the nightmares, the feeling of dread…

For years he'd settled for being numb—outwardly successful, inwardly dead.

Now he was thawing, and the agony it exposed was spreading beyond him.

Everything had changed since this teething ring had been in his possession, and he wanted it back where it belonged.

'Arif thinks I should take it back myself.'

'Go into the jungle?'

'He's offered to take me.'

'Maybe it would help?'

'How? I watched my family disappear before my eyes. Believe me when I say I don't want to relive it.'

It was the first time he'd really spoken about it, and she felt her heart squeeze. 'You saw it?'

'I don't know,' he admitted. 'I guess I must have. I should have stopped it.'

'What were you supposed to do?' she asked. 'What could a child do?'

'Kept him in the boat with me.'

'Hugo?'

'Believe me when I say that I was the adult in that family.'

He was still furious with them; she could feel it.

'I was taken out of school—not just to travel but to take care of him. And I didn't.'

'You can't let guilt stop you living your life.'

'I don't let guilt stop me,' Carter said. 'I've built the life that I want.'

She nodded, but she felt it wasn't enough, that something should be said. But she knew Carter would not have that conversation.

'Anyway,' he said, 'it's a double apology. The reason I came back to the room was to say you were right.' He looked at her. 'I am not used to sharing my day with any other—calling, saying goodbye.'

'I know.'

'I'm new to this, too, Grace.'

She nodded.

'I'll try and call, and I should be back by Sunday.'

'Thank you.'

'Very well, I hope to see you on Sunday.' He looked right into her eyes. 'Preferably with no knickers on...but I'm guessing I'm not allowed to say that.'

He made her laugh even as she pushed him away, even as he blew her a kiss at the door.

'Oh, God,' she said, when he had safely gone.

Grace knew she was in trouble.

Big trouble.

Because she didn't want Carter to lie and pretend that he loved her.

The more time she spent with him, the more she wanted it to be for real.

She couldn't be falling in love with him.

That wasn't the plan…

CHAPTER TWELVE

CARTER'S CONTRITION DIDN'T LAST.

He really was the worst fiancé, even allowing for the fact their engagement was fake.

Not a single call or text.

Even if he was in the desert, there were a couple of airports in between, and when she looked up Sahir and the opulent palace… Oh, she was rather certain there would be the odd occasion when he could call.

But nothing.

So, she'd shopped, as any good Carter Bennett fiancée would.

And Kuala Lumpur was incredible. The shops were airy and beautiful, and the cakes…. Oh, her mother would have loved them. Every afternoon Grace carefully selected a treat and brought one back with her. And she visited the Batu Caves and climbed the coloured stairs, stood at the top and looked out onto the glorious view.

But there was only so much shopping and sightseeing she could do.

And she hated lying to Violet, so their conversations were a little short.

'What's happening with you and that guy?' she'd asked.

'I like him,' Grace said. 'A lot.'

'And?' Violet prompted. 'Does he have a name?'

'Violet…'

'God, you're mean.' She laughed. 'I'll wait for all the gossip when you're home. I popped in to find out how your mum is getting on today.'

'Thanks for that.'

'They're thrilled with her,' Violet said. 'Please don't worry. I peeked in and saw her line dancing…'

Grace laughed. 'I know. I'm trying to buy her a Stetson…'

Grace was still smiling as she took out the folder Arif had given her and read detailed notes about the gradual rise in the number of orangutans on Carter's land, the rare birds they were encouraging, the decline in saltwater crocodiles…

Felicity's work was fascinating—tracking endangered birds, some exclusive to the area—and Grace found herself all too often straying from her task.

Instead of inputting data, she was looking things up. And rather too often she found herself looking up Carter.

It was unsettling to see evidence of his decadent past, and a lot of it seemed rather recent. And it served her right for peeking, because she found out that Sahir was a playboy, and he and Carter had been hitting the social pages since their university days.

She tried not to feel a little tense that he was in the company of the playboy prince now…

It took a lot of scrolling to get further back into his past and when she did, she thought her heart would break.

A miracle. That was what they'd called Carter.

There were pictures of a helicopter, and him being stretchered out.

And Grace, who really didn't cry, wept right there in the hotel's business centre when she saw his scarred face and dark eyes.

Then, in an article a couple of years later, Carter had been photographed standing in a short coat beside a Christmas tree with his glamorous aunt.

She scrolled on, but it didn't help matters. Because there was an image of Carter coming out of a theatre, rumoured to be engaged, and he was with the most beautiful woman Grace had ever seen...

She peered at the date.

Last month!

At that moment, as if he knew she was snooping again, her phone rang and she saw that finally it was him.

'Hey...' She attempted to sound normal. 'How's it going?'

'Stalemate,' Carter said, and let out a breath. 'It's the most beautiful building I've ever worked on, but one wing of the palace was destroyed by an earthquake more than a century ago. We've been going off old plans and drawings, but a lot of the design is based on astronomy—a first for me.' He sounded incredibly tired. 'Most of the council don't even want it done.'

Carter had reverted to his usual tactics and withdrawn—but, given the serious nature of the project, and given that Sahir was a friend, he hadn't simply walked out. Instead he was cooling his heels, sitting in the opulent royal lounge at a private members' club.

'What are you up to now?' Grace asked.

'Watching a sandstorm.'

'Sounds spectacular.'

'From behind glass, it is. Sahir wants to head out...'

He paused, not really wanting to discuss Sahir's methods for solving an issue.

For so long he'd wondered why Sahir would disappear into the desert for days or weeks on end. Yet a part of Carter understood the search for answers.

Those damned dreams now featured Grace, disappearing on a plane, or sinking beneath the water. It was now always Grace rather than his mother holding Hugo, who was gnawing on that teething ring as they walked into the dense forest...

* * *

'Head out?' Grace asked, but he didn't elaborate, and she felt an odd sinking feeling.

They hadn't parted on a row, they'd spoken afterwards and he'd been kind, but she had doubts leaping in her chest like salmon...

'So, what are *you* doing?' he asked.

'I'm trying to find a Stetson for my mother?'

'Excuse me?'

'She's taken up line dancing, apparently...' Grace gave a small laugh. 'I need to find a sparkly shirt and a hat for her. Oh, and I'm working on that data Arif gave me.'

'You don't have to do any of that.'

'I like doing it,' Grace admitted. 'There are reams of information about the conservation work being undertaken. I don't see that Benedict stands a chance if it's taken to court.'

'Careful,' he warned, 'you might put yourself out of a job. I need a wife so I can inherit the property.'

But then his voice changed and he was serious.

'Look, I agree. If it goes to court, we'll eventually win— "eventually" being the operative word. However, there is damage being done now.'

'I know.'

She went quiet, aching to admit just how very nice it was to hear from him. And to tell him that from her digging around in his past she knew the anniversary of his family's deaths was fast approaching. She wondered if it was on his mind. It had to be, she decided, even while knowing the phone wasn't the place to bring up something so deeply personal.

Still, she took a breath. 'It will be nice to go back there.'

'If the talks with Jonathon go well, and the contracts get signed, we soon shall be.'

'For how long?'

'Just for the wedding—one night.'

'We could stay for a bit longer...'

'The point of this marriage is to end my obligations, so I can spend as little time there as possible.'

'I know.' Grace sighed. 'But that doesn't mean I can't go by myself.'

'Excuse me?'

'You've said yourself you'll be away nearly all the time, and I'm enjoying collating the data. I don't mind going.'

'It's data entry,' he snapped. 'You can do that remotely.'

'I like it there, though.' She looked at the meticulous notes spread before her. 'I wouldn't mind getting more involved.'

'You're supposed to be acting as my wife for a year,' he said, pulling rank. 'If I'd wanted Jane Goodall I'd have asked her to marry me. Or Felicity…'

The sound of Grace's laughter down the line actually brought a reluctant smile to his lips.

'I'm not suggesting throwing darts at wildlife and tagging them,' she said.

'Good.'

But despite his smile, he could hear her interest ramping up. A couple of weeks away from the jungle and already she was longing to return. It was all too familiar. His grandfather had never left, and his parents had been drawn back over and over again…

Carter got it.

For all it had taken from him, the place, and the people, the jungle still held a certain allure.

And now Grace was becoming ensnared…

'That type of work is best left to the experts—that's what I'm trying to secure.'

'And my job is to be Carter Bennett's adoring wife?'

'Correct.'

'Carter, about the wedding…'

'What about it?'

'If you want to go out with Arif and take Hugo's teething ring back, I get it…'

'Grace,' he snapped. 'I'm at work.'

Damn. There was a reason he didn't make personal calls. But once he'd rung off he sat staring at the sandstorm, and there was a part of him that wanted to call her back, admit that he was thinking of going…

Hearing Grace talk about Hugo, he'd felt everything coming back to him. That time standing in the boat, watching the mother and baby orangutans disappear, the mangosteens… And he didn't know if it was the teething ring or Grace that was unlocking him.

Or both.

And he didn't know what he was going to find out. Certainly he didn't want witnesses when he faced whatever demons lay waiting there.

But only a local or a fool went into the jungle alone.

Carter was neither.

So that meant things needed to be taken care of.

Places and people too…

He pulled up a name on his phone and called his assistant. 'Tell Jonathon I need him in KL. I want the wedding contract signed and my estate sorted…'

Damn. For someone determined not to care, there was an awful lot to sort out.

He just wanted the teething ring buried…to make his peace with the land, or whatever.

And he knew he had to deal with things the only way he knew how—alone.

And neither Arif nor Grace could know.

CHAPTER THIRTEEN

'HI, HONEY, I'M HOME...'

Grace thought she was hallucinating when Carter appeared three days earlier than her vague expectations—completely unannounced, ever gorgeous in a suit, and wearing a Stetson.

'What on earth...?' She blinked, not just at his unexpected arrival, more at the fact that Carter didn't do 'cheery'. 'I thought you weren't back till Sunday?'

'I got fed up, sitting around waiting. They can call me when they've finished debating. You have no idea how hard this hat was to find in the Middle East. Actually, Ms Hill had it sent to me.' He took it off and placed it on her head. 'For your mother. Though it suits you...'

'Thanks,' Grace said. 'I think.'

He wasn't looking at her, Grace noticed. He was talking, but not actually looking her way, and she had an awful sinking feeling.

He'd been out with Sahir.

And that wasn't just her insecurity talking.

He didn't love her.

He'd told her.

'Also,' he said as he threw off his jacket, 'Jonathon's coming in.'

'When?'

'He should be here soon.'

'Now?' she asked. She was pleased to see Carter, but unsettled by the surprise and the sudden changes. 'I thought that wasn't until Monday?'

'That was the plan, but I might be called back to Janana at any time. It's like waiting for the smoke at the Vatican. We'll just get this marriage contract done…'

'Why?'

'Why not?' He shrugged. 'You have your questions ready?'

'Yes.'

'Then why wait?' he asked, tossing his passport into the safe. 'I want this sorted.'

'But why the sudden rush?' she asked. 'We can't get married for another week, so it's not as if we have a wedding date.' And perhaps she'd been peeking into his scandalous life too much, because she couldn't help but ask, 'Is some scandal about to hit?'

'What are you talking about?'

'I don't know…'

Something had changed, but Grace didn't quite know what. And when he stripped off to shower she found herself looking at his back, his chest, telling herself she was being paranoid.

'It's to your advantage,' he said as he dropped his trousers. 'You get a quarter of a million on signing.'

'I'll remember that,' she said, and smiled, though it faded as he headed off to the shower.

She felt ridiculous for being suspicious, and a bit teary too, and she couldn't work out why. Oh, other than the fact that she was crazy about a playboy who was only marrying her to release some assets.

And today her period was due.

She pulled on her new knickers and bra, floral and lacy this time, and of her own selection. Then she put on a new dress—a gorgeous russet linen that was cinched in at the waist.

'New stylist?' he asked as he came into the bedroom.

'Yes,' Grace said as she glazed her lips orange. 'Me.'

For the first time it was as if he'd actually noticed what she wore, and he ran his fingers through her curls as they were about to head out.

'You look incredible.'

He looked at her, right into her eyes, held her cinched waist and looked at her glossy lips. 'Slatternly…'

'Thanks.' She smiled. 'I think…'

'Come on, then,' Carter said, and they walked together but apart to the elevator.

It was a different room from the one they'd sat in before, and displayed were different flowers—a huge vase of pink orchids was the centrepiece this time.

'It's a late start,' Jonathon said, all polite smiles.

Carter watched as Grace took out her notepad, and he saw about twenty yellow tabs sticking out…

Of course Grace would be taking this seriously.

So too was he.

But he wanted her signature tonight. He wanted this document signed. He wanted them to exist on paper before he went into the jungle.

And if she was pregnant he'd be taking care of that too.

As well as his grandfather's property and land.

Jonathon would be earning his keep tonight.

They went through the financial figures, and all were as arranged before.

'Agreed,' Carter said.

'Grace?' Jonathon checked.

'Agreed.'

'The wedding will take place in Sabah?'

'Agreed,' Carter said.

'Agreed.' Grace nodded. 'However…'

Carter watched as she took a breath, looked at the notes she'd written.

'If this is to appear real, then I'd like to have a small reception. At least let my mother see me.'

'A reception in London?' Jonathon glanced at his main client, who nodded. 'It might help our case with Benedict.'

'Agreed.'

Jonathon went through everything, point by endless point. Grace would receive a quarter of a million on signing the contract, a further sum after the solemnisation of their marriage, followed by serval payments through the year.

The words blurred on the page as Grace was taken through them, her heart pummelled and torn by seeing something that should be beautiful reduced to clauses and subclauses, but she gave nothing away.

Did that make her just as calculated and hard-hearted as Carter?

She hoped so.

She actually hoped that for the next year she would be able to place her emotions in deep freeze, tell herself she was agreeing to this only for the sake of her mum.

But she could think of no other man with whom she could even contemplate doing this.

She fiddled with the ring, just a little loose on her finger, as more intimate details were relayed.

'Agreed,' Carter said, accepting his responsibility for contraception.

'Agreed,' she repeated, and it felt as if they were ticking boxes, racing to get this over and done with.

'Jewellery and gifts…' Jonathon intoned, instructing her to turn the page.

On and on…

There was an offer to break for afternoon tea, and Grace was about to nod when Carter cut in.

'I'd rather push on.'

She felt rushed, and she didn't know why. She felt as if the man who had turned her world upside down a few weeks ago had walked in this morning and upended it all over again…

And then they were done, and a new contract would be drafted.

Only as much as she wanted things wrapped up, Grace wasn't done. 'I do have another question.'

'Of course.'

'What happens if I am pregnant?'

'Have you had a positive test?' Jonathon asked.

'No.'

'Well, let's not deal in hypotheticals.'

'Let's,' Grace said.

Carter closed his eyes. Because while he could sort out the financials, where the rest was concerned he had no answers.

He knew he had to sort out his head.

'Excuse me.'

He stood and let his lawyer deal with that question—exactly the way he would have done three weeks ago, before everything had changed.

They were in there for a full forty minutes, and he saw her pale face when she came out.

'Grace...'

She brushed past him. 'I'm going to have tea up in the suite.'

She could barely look at him.

But it was nothing she didn't already know.

Carter didn't want a baby.

All decisions on a pregnancy would be hers. She'd be provided for financially. If she continued with the pregnancy the baby's way in life would be paved with gold.

Everything he'd told her from the start.

Except she knew him now, and had thought he was better than that.

She couldn't keep it in, turning back on her new heels at the last moment.

'At least my father made *some* attempt.'

She took a breath, trying to get her head around Jonathon's breakdown of the figures around Carter's complete abdication of responsibility.

'Not you, though. Not one piece of that black heart...' She shook her head, her temper rising, and hit her fist into her palm. 'Hit and run.'

'Grace...'

He knew she was hurting, but he didn't want to offer any solution, or tell her he was heading into the jungle and hoping to fix that black heart.

He honestly didn't think there were any answers there, but he would try. He'd bury the teething ring, wish his family peace, or whatever, but he just didn't see that going back to hell would work...

How many times and how many ways had he said it over the decades and years?

He. Did. Not. Want. Love.

Now it was staring him angrily in the face, and he was just a bit angry too.

'Don't compare me to your father, because I shall take care of my child, and you. But not—'

'I get it.' She put her hands up. 'I don't think I can do this...'

'Your period is not even late.' Carter would not let her end things here. 'And we're going for dinner,' he told her.

'With your lawyer and his wife?'

He didn't correct her—didn't tell her that it would only be Jonathon. He just nodded when she gave a bitter smile.

'I might give it a miss, thanks.'

CHAPTER FOURTEEN

IN NO MOOD for candles, Grace flicked on the *Do Not Disturb* light and took off her clothes and curled up in bed.

It was pouring again, the rainwater cascading off the towers and sliding down the glass windows. It looked cold and wintry outside, though she knew it was hot.

The reverse of Carter.

Sitting in that room with Jonathon had hurt, but she'd already pretty much known Carter's take on fatherhood.

And she didn't know if she was angry because he didn't want a baby that might not even exist, or hurting because he could not, would not, did not love her.

It felt back to front to be considering saying no to marriage because she loved the groom—far too much!

Carter didn't exactly rush dinner, and the towers were in darkness by the time he came back to their bedroom.

He saw Grace close her eyes as he undressed.

'I know you're awake,' Carter said.

She didn't answer.

He climbed into bed and lay there for ages.

'Definitely awake...' he said into the dark silence.

He was going back into the jungle to find hope for them, but he might be losing her in the process. Only he didn't know how to reach out. How to explain that he didn't know what he'd find there—or, worse, would come back the same? Closed off and cold. Great for sex and money, just not for the love she silently demanded.

She finally fell asleep. Carter knew because she rolled into him. And he lay there trying to work out the route he'd be taking in the jungle.

Every time he closed his eyes he felt as if he was perched up high, flying over Kuala Lumpur, or high in the jungle, looking for the banyan tree, or some familiar sign…

He snapped his eyes open, felt the relief of her limbs around his and her head on his chest, and he didn't even attempt to lever her off.…

Damn you, Arif.

If the windows here opened he'd take that damn silver teething ring and toss it out now…

He closed his eyes, only he saw his brother again, peering over his mother's shoulder. Hugo's fat hand reaching out. And there was a scream building, his body paralysed as his heart beat a tattoo in his chest, and he shot awake, felt the icy drench of sweat as he gulped in air.

Grace could feel his hand on her arm, and she felt as if her body was a cheat—because it disobeyed her strict orders to turn away, or return to its corner and come out fresh for the next round. She didn't want this fight, if that was what they were having.

'You're lying to me,' Grace said into the dark. 'I don't know about what, I just know that you are.'

'Grace…'

He didn't deny it, instead he silenced he questions the best way he knew how.

For the first time she felt guilty at the pleasure of his kiss— as if her hurt should somehow erase her want.

But not guilty enough to stop.

It was a temporary solution, but she would take the relief, and she sank into him and kissed him back as if they were lovers who'd been parted for a decade. Or strangers who'd met in the dark and would be gone by light.

When he rolled her onto her back she was possibly forgiving them *both* their careless mistake that first night, because she was panting as he sheathed himself, holding the sheet rather than grabbing at him as he rolled it on, and she moaned in relief when he slipped in.

It was eyes closed and private, neither wanting to look at the other as they pushed hurt aside and caved in to desire, and in that Grace knew they were agreed.

She had never thought she could want and feel wanted, could trust another person the way she trusted him when she was in his arms, could feel—for now, at least—together with him in a place they could meet and agree.

'Grace…'

He was not holding back, and he pushed her to new limits. And he made her a noisy lover.

The only thing she held back were the words from her heart. Because she would never, ever say it—never admit it, even as he came deep inside her, even as her body arched and orgasmed at his bidding.

She would deny to his face, if she had to, that this was love.

CHAPTER FIFTEEN

GRACE WOKE TO the sound of Carter dressing, and the snap of the catch on his watch told her he was almost out through the door.

She rolled over in bed and watched as he pulled on his tie. He barely glanced over as he spoke.

'The council in Janana has called us in.'

'When will you be back?'

'I'm not sure.'

'I wish we hadn't had sex last night,' she told him.

'Really?'

'No…' Grace admitted. 'But I don't think I want this marriage. I don't think I can fake it for a year.'

'Fake what?' he asked, with all the confidence of someone who knew she wasn't lying when she was in bed with him.

Then, to her quiet surprise, he came and sat on the bed, took her hand and looked at the ring.

'Listen to me. On your phone you should have the new contract.' He picked it up and handed it to her. 'Check.'

She squinted. 'Yes.'

'Sign it,' he said. 'We'll work out dates as soon as I'm back.'

'I don't know…'

'Stay till I get back?' He gave her thigh a squeeze through the sheet. 'We could have a very nice year.'

He kissed her on the cheek, and then he looked right into

her eyes. And she knew that fifty years from now, if she met that gaze, he would melt her again.

He kissed her both deeply and nicely, and she breathed him in as he held her. 'If I do leave, I'm stealing your cologne.'

'I've got to go.'

'I hope the council approves.'

He smiled, and then he was gone, and she realised she could lie in bed for an eternity and still be no closer to working him out.

She should get up and shower and then go to a pharmacy... buy a pregnancy test and find out once and for all.

Unless it was too soon.

Or there was nothing to find out.

Grace bought her first pregnancy test kit and then came back to the hotel, but she had to wait for room service to finish before she dared used it.

She came out of the bathroom and willed herself to wait the requisite minutes.

Of course she paced.

And then she glanced at the open-plan shelving near the entrance.

Carter had forgotten his plans.

She took her phone out to text him, wondering if he'd boarded yet, or was about to dash back through the door, or send someone more likely.

But then she stood stock-still.

He surely wouldn't forget the blueprints.

Even on the boat, deep in kisses, he'd made sure to drag them to and from the house. Even the first time they'd met he'd been holding them.

She called him and got sent straight to Ms Hill. 'I'd like to speak with Carter.'

'Mr Bennett's unavailable. I can pass on a message.'

'He's left his blueprints.'

'I'll let him know.'

She sounded utterly unperturbed, and as Grace took a breath it dawned on her that possibly he hadn't forgotten his plans...

For someone who'd been caught red-handed before, Grace didn't hesitate to punch the numbers into the safe.

Yes, his passport was gone. But what made her swallow was the fact that the black pouch was missing too.

Her heart was fluttering in her throat, panic building, and she wasn't quite sure why. It was just that it was the anniversary in two days, and she knew he wanted that teething ring back where he thought it belonged.

Carter had been lying to her.

He wasn't heading to Janana. He was going into the jungle...

Her hands were shaking as she went through the folder, took out the card and called Arif. But his number kept ringing out.

In the end she called Felicity.

'Arif's at a conference,' she said, all efficient and cheery. 'He should be back at the weekend.'

'You're sure he's at a conference?'

'He's the guest speaker.' Felicity gave a jolly laugh. 'So I really hope so.'

Grace shook her head. 'I thought Carter was meeting with him?'

'Not that I've heard.'

He was going alone.

Grace sat on the bed. Her head was all jumbled, and yet she was utterly certain that Carter was returning the teething ring.

Alone.

He would never go with Arif—she could see that now.

Nor would he go with her.

There were some pains so private you dealt with them alone.

She thought about how she'd shut Violet out rather than tell her what was going on at home. How there were some things you didn't want others to see. And yet they wanted to be there…

She looked at her ring and was taken back to the fireflies and that wonderful night…and the tension in Carter, the flashlight skimming the water.

And, no, she couldn't go with him—he wouldn't want her to, that much was clear.

But she could be there waiting for him.

The biggest problem she'd thought she had had been relegated, but it was remembered now and, feeling oddly calm, she walked back into the gorgeous bathroom.

Yes, she was going to be a mum.

Only Carter didn't want to be a dad.

But she'd tell him anyway.

To his face.

She'd never once regretted telling her mother she loved her.

It was time to tell Carter the same.

Even if he didn't want her.

They deserved a proper goodbye.

CHAPTER SIXTEEN

CARTER COULD HAVE approached from the river, sat in the safety of the boat and tossed the teething ring in, but he'd never been going to do that.

And so he'd taken the long way, setting off at dawn and approaching the river from his grandfather's property, retracing the steps he had taken with Arif as a child.

Although the incident had taken place further up river from where they'd used to turn around and head home.

A lot further.

Hot, humid, dense…

He hated the place, and every step was taking him closer to a place he didn't feel he needed to be.

He reached the spot where Bashim had found him, but he knew that only from what he'd been told. There was nothing he could remember here.

Or maybe a little…

Hot…thirsty…his head throbbing…

He walked further in and he could hear the chirps and sounds of the jungle. Looking up, he knew he'd climbed a tree, his limbs aching, pulling his puny body up. Searching for the banyan tree…knowing he was lost.

He also saw the spot where he'd fallen.

He recalled the taste of blood, and remembered he'd known he had to stem it…

Some were his own memories, some were Bashir's tales, but nothing helped.

Yet as he got closer his pace picked up.

He was following the line of the river, but well back from the mangroves.

And he'd been right, Carter decided, when he saw the silvery striped mangroves. Even if he'd done his best to avoid this spot, he knew it exactly. Yet there were no answers to be had here.

This place that had tormented him for a lifetime was not the stuff of nightmares.

Birds flashed like red jewels, and where the dense canopy of trees thinned there were glimpses of cloudy blue skies.

As Carter drank the last of the water he'd brought, he decided it had been a mistake to come.

Hunger gnawed. He picked up a mangosteen and stared at it, then tossed it away, deciding he would never be that hungry again.

Yet he bent to retrieve it, and as he held the rough waxy orb the desperation he'd felt as a child was revived…the fatigue and hunger as he'd bashed it on a stone, the purple wax seeping in, the usually sweet white parcels stained and rotten, bitter on his tongue.

Yet he'd eaten them.

No wonder he couldn't stand them now.

He took one and peeled it open, saw the pretty white parcels like the ones he'd opened for Grace that beautiful morning. He thought of that cocktail, and how she'd simply put it down when he told her.

She'd brushed her teeth before she'd kissed him—and that memory felt like her smile.

He tasted the fruit and it was sweet…like peaches.

He tossed it away.

The heat and the low-hanging branches made it a fight at times to move even a few steps further. His shirt was torn, a heavy branch swung back, and he felt the tear of the flesh on his cheek. He reached for his water bottle, but of course it was long empty, and he knew he was on his own with the elements. But still he was not concerned. This had been his and Arif's playground. The boys had often gone further than his grandfather would have permitted, and it had been a regular outing throughout the summer, with overnight treks a frequent adventure. Even a couple of nights at times.

They'd always stopped here, though.

Arif would put out his arm and halt them, telling Carter they should go no further.

'But the river is just through there...' Carter would protest, for it was just a couple of miles ahead, and he'd known someone there might give them a ride back, or take them to their home for a meal.

But Arif had always pointed to the still, shallow stretch of water, sometimes high from recent rain. 'Mortal danger.'

Even at eight years old, Carter had known what that meant.

'Idiot!' he muttered, his lip curling on the word.

For how the hell had his father thought it safe to bring his family here? To watch as his wife carried his infant into infested waters?

He came to the edge of the mangroves, their silver branches like bony arms stretching skywards, beyond the river. They looked eerie, yet beautiful in the pale moonlight, and he scanned the water for the glint of eyes or any movement. But it was peaceful. And there was a rope over the river that hadn't been there when he was a child, put there for the orangutans.

It had been dusk when his mother had said she wanted to take the perfect photo—to capture the setting sun and the little kingfisher perched over the water.

'Sophie!'

He could hear his father warning her to stay back, telling her that the water in the mangroves was deep from a week of torrential rain.

It was comparatively dry now, but he looked at the water and knew the dangers that lurked beneath. He stood there numb, refusing to feel, but it was as if he was witnessing again the stealth of the beast approaching.

He'd attempted to shout—'No!' But the sound of the word hadn't carried, and his mother had suddenly plunged lower in the water, as if she'd stepped off a ledge.

He felt again his relief when she'd seemed to right herself, rising up in the water again.

Then he'd heard one desperate shout from his father, seen the whipping water his father had rushed towards.

And now, as he had all those years ago, Carter stood horror-struck and silent, watching, waiting for his father to sort this out, to save his mother, for she and Hugo to emerge.

Apart from that single shout from his father there had been no screams, no noise, when surely there should have been?

The thrashing, beating water had gone still.

Carter had gone in.

He felt again that blind panic. Holding his breath…searching the water…shouting to his father who lay face-down, urging him to help find Hugo…

'Papa!' He'd urged him to wake up. 'Hugo… Ulat…'

His hand had closed on something, and he'd frantically pulled—but it had just been roots and leaves, and he'd screamed to his father again. 'Find him!'

Even then there had been the first stirrings of anger at his father, who lay motionless and incapable of helping find his son. Anger at his impetuous mother, who had stepped out of the boat without thought or care for the precious infant in her arms.

At some level he'd known his mother was dead, but he'd told himself the baby would have slipped out of the sling, that Ulat would rise, smiling like he did when they played in the pool. Surely? After all, there was no blood in the water…no sign that anything had occurred.

Then he'd looked to his father, still face-down, his arms spread, and it had been then that Carter had realised he stood in infested water.

His own sense of survival, the lessons from long days spent in the jungle with Arif, had kicked in.

Mortal danger.

He'd waded out, still searching the water with his hands, scanning the muddy edges for Hugo, calling out to him, unable to fathom that he was gone.

All of them were gone.

Gone.

He'd never cried, or screamed, and he didn't now. He just sat there feeling again the winter, and the emptiness, the finality. And that was the part of the nightmare he never wanted to get to.

No, he hadn't run for help. He'd wandered, dazed, knowing they were gone for ever.

And he'd loved them—his floaty mother, his hapless father, their passion and their slight craziness...

He thought of his father, his brief eye-roll before he'd called out to stop his wife. But it would have been like trying to halt the wind. Her passion, her longing for adventure, had been impossible to contain.

Carter's anger was misdirected. It wasn't at his family, nor even the animals who had simply been being true to their nature.

It was at himself.

He hadn't stopped them, hadn't called out, and he'd failed to protect his baby brother. Little Hugo, who had brought so much delight into the world, who in the chaos of a somewhat nomadic existence had, for Carter, been like a little beacon. Hugo's routine had been a welcome dose of normality in a disorderly existence.

His heart thumped in his chest. And now there was nothing to show for his existence.

One thing.

Carter pulled the silver teething ring from his pocket and opened the pouch. His intention was to somehow return Hugo's beloved teething ring, his comfort, to him. He saw the little teeth marks…and now he ran a finger over them and cried the tears he never had before.

It was the teething ring that had caused this. This place had been calling to him the night he'd been with Grace…

And now Carter knew why he was here.

Love had returned to his life even when he'd tried to deny it had ever existed.

A bird landed on a branch—a blaze of colour in the silver and grey—and, yes, all these years on he knew it was the kingfisher his mother had hoped to capture in her photo.

He looked down at the silver teething ring, at the scratched surface, and thought of Hugo's bright smile, how trusting he'd been…

His milky breath and gurgles of laughter.

His contented smile.

Contentment…

He thought of Grace…how she was terrified of being forgotten by those she loved.

'You'll never be forgotten, Hugo,' he said aloud.

He wouldn't let a single memory fade for as long as his life allowed.

He could almost hear his brother's bright smiling laughter and, pocketing the treasure, he knew now where he was headed…where he'd been trying to get all those years ago.

He had been going home.

CHAPTER SEVENTEEN

'*SELAMAT.*'

Arif offered peace as he greeted him, just on the edge of dawn.

'*Selamat,*' Carter said. 'I thought you were away…?'

'I heard you were back…'

And, like a friend, he'd dropped everything the moment he'd found out.

It had taken Carter a full twenty-four hours to get back, and he'd eaten more of that damn fruit—but thankfully not rotten this time. Or was it that the world was a bit sweeter this day?

'You need to bathe,' Arif said. 'Eat…'

'Sleep?'

'Soon.'

And as Carter ate a light meal he was grateful that he did not ask how it had been.

Only as Malay cleared his plate did Arif tell him he was in trouble. 'You left the plans behind.'

He frowned.

'Your blueprints. Grace was calling everyone…'

He would have to come up with a suitable lie, Carter decided.

Or simply tell her the truth about where he'd been.

'She's asleep,' Arif told him.

'Who?'

'Grace,' Arif said, and told him his brother had picked her up last night.

'She's here?'

'Pacing all day.' Arif smiled. 'I told her to get some rest, that you might not be back till tomorrow. You made good time.'

'You mean she's here now?'

'In your residence.'

Carter wasn't sure if he was sleepwalking, or if he was having some delusion and would wake with a fever, but this was not like the last time. He felt invigorated, rather than collapsed. Curious, rather than frantic, as he walked through his part of the property.

Climbing the stairs, he found he wasn't avoiding the pictures now. He could see his parents smiling, and Hugo too.

Then he pushed open his bedroom door and indeed Grace was there, lying on her back, wearing a muslin nightdress, the fan blowing.

He could not quite believe she had followed him here.

That she was waiting at his home.

And then he could—because he knew she loved him or he'd never have come here.

She was still wearing the ring.

'Grace…' He sat on the bed, and this time when he reached for her slender shoulder he did not pull his hand back. 'Grace!'

Her eyes shot open, and so did her mouth, but she said nothing, just wrapped herself around him, coiled around him, more sweet pea than bindweed.

'I thought you were dead…'

'You were having a very good sleep,' he teased, holding her and breathing her in. 'Perhaps you fell unconscious with panic?'

'Stop!' She pulled back. 'You lied…'

'I did—but I had to.'

* * *

'No.'

She wanted to tell him it didn't work like that—except he'd climbed into bed and, given it was *his* bed, she couldn't really refuse him entry.

'I'd have come with you.'

He shook his head, tried to explain, but Grace had been waiting a long time to say what she'd come here to say.

'I know you don't want anyone, but...'

She'd thought he had died every moment since she'd seen the plans he had left behind, and her biggest regret was the one thing she hadn't told him.

'I love you. I'm sorry, and I know you don't want to hear it...' She put her hands up when it looked as if Carter might say something. 'But let me speak. I want you to know that. And I want to say a proper goodbye.'

'Why would you come all this way to say goodbye?'

'Because goodbyes are important.'

'I know,' he told her. 'But this was never about goodbye, Grace.'

Carter lay down and the bed was like a pillow, and then she was running her fingers over his eyes, and his scratches, and he was aware of just her fresh air scent.

'I hated the thought of you here,' he told her. 'I didn't want you on a jungle walk... I didn't want you coming back...'

'Don't be—'

'I mean it. I hated the thought of you here... I had to go into the jungle to find out that I don't hate the land, and I don't blame my parents. I thought I did, and I even hated myself. But I didn't know what I feared till now.'

She looked at him.

'It was losing another person I love to this place.'

'You love me?'

'From the moment we met.'

'No, from the night we came here.'

She kissed his dry mouth and then she got up, and he lay still as she put orange gloss on his parched lips.

He shook his head. 'The moment we met,' he confirmed. 'I felt obliged to go over to you...obliged to pick up your passport—the same way I feel obliged to this place. I think it's a little like love.'

'No...'

'Sometimes it seems that way,' he insisted.

And she breathed, and he nodded, because there were obligations, and some were hard to keep, but when you loved someone you stepped up.

'I couldn't tell them apart,' Carter admitted. 'Obligations and love. I didn't want to tell them apart. But I know for certain this is love.'

Grace rested her head on his chest. He loved her—she knew that from his kiss, from the way he held her for a full moment, just breathing together.

But then another wave of panic at what might have been hit.

'You could have died.' She said it again. 'Even Arif was worried.'

'Grace, I've been dead for almost thirty years. I haven't felt a damn thing since I watched them all disappear.'

Now he felt everything. This sensory overload, this pain, the fear, the warmth of her smile...

His kiss was rough and yet tender. He felt the scratch of his unshaven jaw, his swollen lips, and then the balm of her tongue.

'Grace, I had to get my head straight.'

He lifted her hand and looked at the ring, then at the woman who had chosen the cheapest ring in the box.

'Fireflies over diamonds?'

'Every time.'

'Marry me?' he asked. 'Not because of this place, and not to take care of your mother.'

He saw her close her eyes.

'I shall take care of your mother whatever your answer. I shall fight Benedict through the courts. I am asking you to marry me because I love you, and because I believe you love me.'

'Would that change if I told you I was pregnant?'

'Not one single bit,' he said. 'And as for all I said before, I regret every word. *Are* you pregnant?'

Grace nodded, scared not of his reaction but because it was all so new.

All of it. Being in love, being loved, being pregnant...

'It's too soon,' she said.

'Would it help if I told you I am brilliant with babies?'

She looked at him.

'I got up to Hugo all the time. We would laugh and sing...'

He reached over and handed her the silver teething ring.

'I adored him...he was the light of this place. And now we're going to have our own Ulat.'

She smiled and examined the teething ring. 'What about its teeth?'

He laughed—he'd clearly worried about the same.

'How soon can we marry?' Grace asked.

'I'm not sure of the rules in London.' He smiled. 'I'll ask my PA.'

'I meant how soon can we get married *here*?'

He frowned, clearly unsure what day it was.

'Twenty-one days after the application.'

'That's today.' She looked at him. 'We can marry today...'

EPILOGUE

IT WAS TO be the tiniest wedding, with a small celebration to follow when they returned to London.

At least, that was what Grace assumed.

The hotel staff, when they'd packed for her, had included the strappy oatmeal linen dress, and it was gorgeous to slip on,

Her hand was shaking as she tried to tie her hair, but Malay came in and helped her twist it and pin in a water hyacinth.

'Everything is ready.' Malay smiled at her. 'How romantic to get married at sunset…'

'I shan't be long.'

She picked up her phone. Gosh, this was going to be a surprise.

'Violet!'

'Grace, you look—' Violet stopped. 'Oh, my God, I don't even know his name. Grace, you cannot get married. Honestly. Whatever—'

'Violet…' Grace gave her dear friend a smile. 'I love you, and we're going to have a proper reception in a few weeks.'

'Grace…' Violet gave in then. 'I'll be here for you.'

'I know.' Grace smiled. 'And I love you for it.'

She took the stairs and saw Jamal, dressed in pale shimmering pink. She handed her some flowers.

'Don't be nervous,' she said.

'I'm not,' Grace said, but then her hand went to her chest. 'Perhaps a little…'

Or was it just excitement? They walked towards the ancient ballroom, but as she stepped in she saw, instead of Carter, the French doors wide open.

'Your groom is waiting for you outside...'

She stepped out and gasped. The pool was lit, and the pathway too, all the trees dotted with lights, and she walked with Jamal through the beautiful grounds to an ancient banyan tree where Carter stood waiting.

And he was so loved... For it wasn't such a small wedding after all—there were many of the local people, dressed exquisitely, playing soft music, as she walked to be by his side.

'How did you do that?' Carter asked, and kissed her. 'Do you travel with a wedding dress?'

He made her laugh, and they kissed again before they were man and wife.

'You look perfect,' he told her.

And for someone who had spent three decades numb, Carter could never have envisaged being surrounded by so much love.

He knew there was no one else he could have shared this with.

The gorgeous tree, the scents and the moonlit sky, and the sounds of the jungle settling for the night. The caws of birds, the chatter of monkeys, and then a certain quiet, as if thousands of eyes were watching them.

The celebrant welcomed everyone in both English and the local dialect, and Carter translated when needed.

And then he took a breath.

'Bashim, Arif's father, is going to speak...' Carter told her, and watched as Arif helped his father to the front.

The man who had searched for a missing boy and carried him home.

Carter's voice was husky as he translated. 'He says that no one is ever lost here...that souls remain...' He squeezed her hands and she squeezed it back. *'Gotong royong,'* Carter said. 'It means life is lighter if we share the burden together.'

And now it was Carter who wanted to speak.

'Grace…' He thought for a moment. 'This morning, when I saw the sunrise, I knew I wanted to spend the rest of my life with you… To come back home and find you waiting here for me was the greatest gift of my life. I shall never stop loving you.'

She believed it,

'Carter…'

She looked up at the man who had claimed her heart the day he had woken her to hand back her passport.

'I have loved you from the moment I laid eyes on you…'

She would never forget opening her eyes to this man, and knowing, somehow, that he was the one for her.

'You have my love.'

For ever…

That was how long true love lasted.

* * * * *

Were you swept off your feet by Bride Under Contract? *Then you'll love these other passion-fueled stories by Carol Marinelli!*

The Greek's Cinderella Deal
Forbidden to the Powerful Greek
The Sicilian's Defiant Maid
Innocent Until His Forbidden Touch
Virgin's Stolen Nights with the Boss

Available now!